Cell Wars

The Battle For Brian

Adam Fox

Published by Electric Light Fiction (ELF) 2011

Copyright © Alistair Forrest (writing as Adam Fox)
ISBN 978-0-9570063-0-0

The author has asserted his moral right under the Copyright, Designs and Patents Act 1988 to be identified as the author of this work. All Rights reserved. No part of this publication may be reproduced, copied, stored in a retrieval system, or transmitted, in any form or by any means, without the prior written consent of the copyright holder, nor be otherwise circulated in any form of binding or cover other than that in which it is published and without a similar condition being imposed on the subsequent purchaser.

A CIP catalogue record for this title is available from the British Library.

Cell Wars is a work of fiction: neither the author nor the publisher accept any responsibility for the actions of individuals upon reading the ideas and concepts contained within this novel.

Cover Design: Lynda Adlington

For our children Sebastian, Simone, Cassie, Corrine and Max

By the same author

www.alistairforrest.com

Libertas (2009) ISBN 978-1906836078

Goliath (2010) ISBN 978-1452327495

Health Commentary: www.best-health-juicing.com

1

Bill needed a holiday.

Well, the word *needed* was probably a little strong. Deserved? Hardly. He wasn't lazy and he wasn't what you might call industrious. But he did his job whenever it needed doing. In his own time.

The head of any department should have a holiday whenever he bloody well pleases, thought Bill and, to emphasise the point he had just made to himself, put his bone china teacup a little too firmly on its saucer.

Startled, the cat leapt from his lap and disappeared behind Bill's untidy desk. The cat had no name and, apparently, no fixed abode. It wasn't his but he occasionally fed it with a digestive biscuit, an act of kindness for which the cat gave no appreciation.

Freed from the unwanted encumbrance, Bill heaved himself out of his armchair and shrugged himself into his faithful tweed jacket, absently noting that the leather elbow patches were wearing thin and only the top button of three remained.

Perhaps a little tatty for the Head of Immigration and Foreign Object Office.

Bill preferred the full title but everyone, including the Chief, referred to the department as IFOO, pronounced *if-foo*, which invariably prompted a po-faced 'Bless You' in response.

Disrespectful and unbecoming of such a well-organised and successful department.

He promised himself that the only work he would do during his holiday would be to think of a completely new and hopefully snappier title for his department. Move with the times. Something with 'Agency' in the title. Foreign Agency maybe, let them try to mess with that.

It wasn't far to the Chief's office. Next door in fact.

Imelda was a large woman whose flowery dresses, Bill suspected, covered the evidence of time. He tried not to think of the dimpled, sagging posterior or the grey elasticated knickers concealed by acres of pleated rayon. Adorned with the strangest mix of roses and gladioli.

It was difficult not to look at the expanse of bottom as The Chief balanced precariously on her antique desk while flapping at an offending fly with a rolled up copy of last week's *Liver Central* report. Best use for it, Bill thought mischievously.

He cleared his throat.

'Ah, Bill,' said Imelda without taking her eye off the insect. 'Be a love and throw something at that fly. It's rather distracting, can't follow my train of thought.'

Imelda's train of thought was her most beautiful attribute, in Bill's opinion. Rarely relevant thoughts, at least as far as The Host was concerned, but beautiful thoughts nonetheless.

He removed a shoe and threw it in the general direction of the fly, missing. But the fly saw sense in beating a hasty retreat when a size eleven is hurled, and disappeared through the office door that Bill had left open.

4

'There,' said Bill, retrieving his shoe if only to cover the hole in his sock through which a yellowing toenail poked menacingly.

'Thank you poppet.' Imelda lowered her bottom onto the desk and slid without grace and dignity to firmer ground. She smiled – another appealing characteristic. 'Now then, what can I do for you, Bill?'

'Well, I…' Bill was not one for getting straight to the point.

'You're still worried about The Host, aren't you?'

'Hmmm. The Host is 63. He's getting old. He's been lucky and so have we–'

'You mean we've had an easy life?' Imelda sounded indignant.

'We've had no crises. No big operations, no sudden heart attacks, only that time when–'

'When The Host choked on a peanut? Lordy, that was scary…'

Bill wrung his hands and looked thoughtful. 'Don't you think, I mean… shouldn't we–'

'Be doing more?' Imelda interrupted, her eyebrows almost meeting.

'Yes.'

'Like what? We haven't had any warning lights in the control room, have we?'

'No, but…'

'But what? Come on Bill, what's this about?'

'Well, I was thinking...' Bill had a habit of not finishing his sentences.

Imelda stared at him, challenging him to complete a simple function that seemed beyond most men.

Bill obliged.

'Well, I was thinking that I might take a short holiday.'

Imelda looked as though she was about to burst into sudden, uncontrolled laughter but she bit her lip and looked straight into Bill's eyes.

'Bill, we are talking about *your* concerns over The Host's age and all that goes with it, liver disease, prostate problems, getting up in the night to pee, his inability to remember even the most basic things of yesteryear – why, he even forgot the vicar's name at the tea party yesterday! And now you are asking me to sign a holiday chit so you can swan off some-where when all hell *could* be about to break loose?'

'Yes,' said Bill, then coughed because he thought his voice had too squeaky a timbre. 'Yes, yes indeed, but it will be a working holiday. I'll go south, straight past Liver Central and check things out.'

'I see.'

'But please don't ask me to check the... the, er, you know... the functional bits. I really couldn't face that on holiday.'

Imelda blushed.

'I mean, Liver Central is bad enough with all that bile and stuff they produce down there, and I don't think that home brew has done The Host any good at all...'

'All right.'

'And those curries he's taken a shine to...'

'I said all right, Bill.'

'You mean...'

'Yes, Bill, you haven't had a holiday in... well *ever* I suppose. I don't imagine you've even got a pair of shorts. Wouldn't want to bare those unseemly knees...'

It was Bill's turn to blush. His knees were of the knobbliest kind, and his legs were embarrassingly thin. No one but Bill himself had ever seen them as far as he could recall.

'Right then,' he mumbled. 'I'll be off then.'

'Before you go, be a darling and fix this monitor. It's the link from Liver Central. On the blink.'

Bill looked at the monitor. It was lifeless, and he knew that where matters of technology were concerned, his brain was just as useless.

'Tell you what,' he blustered, turning for the still open door to follow the fly from Imelda's lair, 'I'll be there tomorrow, and I'll come straight back if I find any, er, problems.'

'Right. You do that. Waste Management Needs You.'

It was a joke, the best Imelda could manage, but Bill was gone without so much as the expected chuckle.

7

2

Nadia seemed to grow more beautiful every time Bill had the good fortune to ask for a transport chitty.

A "chitty" was the quaint terminology for what was, in effect, a train ticket of sorts. Transport cost nothing, especially for the Head of IFOO or a Chief like Imelda. It was always dispensed by the lovely Nadia with her olive skin, fine (if a little long) nose, big brown eyes and jet-black hair that seemed to change hue like a waterfall every time she shifted position. The faintest twitch of her goddess's head sent a quiver along every fibre and a shiver down Bill's spine, reminding him at the shiver's end that he was still a man.

'Going south, Sir?' asked Nadia ever so suggestively.

'Indeed.' Bill's ubiquitous strait-laced reply. He would be well into his journey before he realised the missed opportunity.

'Will you be long?'

Another missed opportunity: 'Two days. IFOO meets on Wednesday.'

'I see.' Nadia sighed. 'Change at Heart Junction for the 1806 to Liver Central. You'll be needing a suit then?'

If there was one regret out of many missed opportunities, it was that Bill did not possess his own transport suit. A messy business going south. The standard-issue units leaked like sieves.

'Please.'

'Size?'

'Medium.' Another opportunity went flashing away from him before he could retrieve it.

Nadia's long legs took her to the stores and she returned with a medium travel suit. It looked like it had clung to the pallid flesh of many an adventurer before him.

'Thank you, Nadia-ah.'

Nadia beamed at him because the charming old gentleman had stretched out the last syllable of her name, giving it an *aitch*, thus betraying his total subservience to her. Few men in this cramped environment gave her the respect she felt was due, let alone expressed any semblance of desire.

He sighed, and left for the pod station.

Bill had a headache.

Being thrust along claustrophobic tubes in a bloodline pod was nothing short of hellish. You can't move, scratch your head or adjust tight underpants in a pod.

The change at Heart Junction gave only momentary relief, and then only to stretch his legs, because the continual pounding was oppressive: *thump THUMP, thump THUMP, thump THUMP.* He made a mental note to tell the Chief that everything seemed normal, at least as far as he could see, even the eerie light that one moment glowed deep red, the next a brilliant yellow, then almost green, affecting his stride as if caught in the mysterious ebb and flow of some great ocean.

He found his southbound pod obediently waiting for him, all cleaned and scrubbed with a curled sandwich placed on the console.

He pressed the green button.

He did not touch the sandwich.

The pod slowed after what could only have been twenty minutes by Bill's foggy reckoning. This gave him the opportunity to observe the palling miasma, the unmistakable drag of thick crimson, the bump and bash of unwanted clots, even the swift-passing shouts of dismay from the tube's maintenance workers.

'Not my fault,' Bill yelled as a fist thumped on the pod's screen as it passed a team of turbaned labourers. They were left behind as he shouted in despair: 'I can't control the bloody thing, don't you know that?'

This isn't right, he thought. It wasn't like this in the old days.

The pod didn't make it as far as Liver Central. Bill climbed out into a quagmire of sticky goo, every step making a sucking sound like wet ground too oft trodden by the same pig.

He heard voices in the distance and made for them.

'Excuse me, which way is Liver Central?'

The three men, all of them overweight with fat faces that squeezed eyes too close together, stopped work as one. And stared at Bill as if he was an insignificant insect.

He wondered if they were foreigners – Liver Central folk were to a man warm, friendly types like Ahmed, the foreman at Liver and Digestive System (LADS for short).

He asked the question again, slowly.

One of them grunted, another shifted the shovel in his hands as if it was a weapon, and the third wiped his nose with the back of his filthy hand. They all wore boiler suits with the trousers tucked into Wellington boots, but it was difficult to discern their ethnic colour such was the muck and grime that covered them.

The worker with a shovel pointed the wide end along a tunnel that branched into even deeper gloom than that in which they stood.

'How far, if you please?' asked Bill in his politest tone. He sensed trouble, a feeling that was completely alien in his pleasant world of IFOO and Imelda's beautiful thoughts, yet it was one that told him he should move on down the tunnel no matter how horrid underfoot.

It was difficult passing the three maintenance men and they smelled foul, like a corked Pinot Noir, but he managed it thanks to his skinny frame.

He didn't look back and lengthened his stride, his suit leaking dreadfully at both ankles, the fumes making it hard to breathe. He tried whistling *The Grand Old Duke Of York* through his teeth but that meant more frequent intake of the reeking air.

Some holiday.

Perhaps things would improve when he found Ahmed and the boys at LADS who always welcomed their seniors with joviality and warm beer.

When he saw the soft yellow glow in the distance, he knew Liver Central could not be far, a chance to hopefully wash away the disgusting grime and put the world to rights.

He pressed on, unaware that The Host had just decided to shrug away a hangover and the effects of a particularly nasty curry with a brisk walk on The Downs.

3

Ahmed was not the same Ahmed.

His laughing eyes were now hooded as if trying to conceal the despair that had stealthily bound and gagged his hitherto generous and happy disposition. His long hair was lank and unwashed, his face gaunt, his shirt grubby and his trousers no longer bore Ahmed's trademark knife-edge crease from thigh to foot.

And his shoelaces were undone.

Bill pushed back his Lycra hood as he entered. 'Ahmed?'

Ahmed looked up from the printout he had been studying. Bio-analysis, thought Bill as he glimpsed the pages of figures. Enough to get anyone down, even Ahmed.

The younger man forced a smile, the effort not lost on Bill who had spent a lifetime studying the reactions of staff under duress. Though these days duress came with a capital D, it seemed.

Bill took a chair opposite Ahmed's desk. 'Are you all right? You look done in.'

'Yeah... yeah, man. Fine. You don't look so good yourself.'

'Well it's mucky out there, worse than ever. Pod didn't quite make it to your door. Don't suppose you have any tea on the go, do you?'

'Oh Sorry. Where are my manners? Tea… yes I think so.'
He rummaged among the sheaves of papers until he found a
teabag hidden under a large book entitled *Clonorchis Sinensis - An Encyclopaedia of the Human Liver Fluke.*

'Well I have a teabag but the kettle's broken,' said Ahmed,
holding it up by its string as if both men should inspect it,
perhaps will it to turn to two mugs of tea all by itself.

'Never mind, old chap. Perhaps we could go for a drink instead…?'

Ahmed shook his head. 'Too much to do here. Bit of a crisis
on.'

'Crisis? Ahmed, what's going on? You don't look well.'

For a moment, Ahmed looked as though he might cry but he
pulled himself together. He rubbed his bloodshot eyes.

'Tell me, Ahmed.'

'It's that bloody canteen where The Host works. Sending
down all this *shite*. Sorry Bill, didn't mean to swear, but
there's no other word for it, all supermarket white bread, hot
dogs, pies and those stupid fizzy sodas… sugar, salt, grease
and *shite*. We're drowning in muck down here, Bill.'

'But I thought –'

'Yes we *all* thought a little bit here and there wouldn't do
any harm, but it's constant now Bill. Bloody constant. Day
in day out. The Host has lost it, he works like a Trojan all
day and grabs a MacSomething on his way home, misses all
those wonderful dinners his wife used to make him. It can't
go on, Bill. It can't.'

'He's not… not *unwell* is he?'

'You bet your sweet bippy he's unwell. He's making us all ill down here. And that godawful home brew...'

Bill leaned back and threw his hands in the air. 'But he's an accountant. A simple accountant by the name of Brian Davis of The Poplars, Watford. What can he know about health? Dammit, he doesn't even know where his liver is let alone what you all do down here.'

'But isn't that *your* job?' Ahmed realized he was being harsh, so he softened his tone. 'Well, I mean, The Chief's job? Help feed The Host's conscience from time to time?'

As if on cue, just as Ahmed had spoken the word "conscience", the room suddenly lurched to one side, and as the upheaval was about to tip both men from their chairs, heaved itself in completely the opposite direction. The effect was temporarily disconcerting, though both Ahmed and Bill knew what was happening.

Brian Davis of The Poplars, Watford, senior partner at Grimson, Ramsbotham and Davis, chartered accountants, had decided upon a brisk walk as a token nod to the advice of his doctor about the need for exercise.

'Don't... need... this... right... now,' hissed Ahmed as he tried unsuccessfully to prevent his papers spilling to the floor while clinging to the desk.

Bill had taken a turn for the worse as the combination of the fetid stench of his journey and the sudden jolting made him feel quite nauseous. He said nothing, just threw himself onto the desk, one hand gripping the edge, the other holding Ahmed's sleeve in a vain attempt to recover stability.

From the corner of his eye he registered a console of flashing lights as all manner of emergencies seemed to erupt simultaneously in the complex corridors of The Host's nether regions, while those that were wired for sound emitted a discordant combination of klaxons and sirens, none of which helped either man in his struggle for dignity and a sense of well-being.

Even when the pitching settled into a slightly gentler rolling motion, they remained for some time lying side by side on the unstable desk, clutching both its ornate if dirt-ingrained antique carvings and each other. They were in this inglorious position when a look of alarm crossed Ahmed's face.

'What?' managed Bill.

'Listen,' replied Ahmed rolling his eyes in the direction he could only assume was upwards.

Bill listened.

There it was, a distinctive low rumbling like the first warnings of Vesuvius awakening.

'Hell, not now,' muttered Ahmed.

'Not what?'

'You'll see. He's away out of the gate, down the street and in open country. In his own little world where nobody will notice.'

'Notice what?'

Bill had his answer when, from the caverns of The Host's stomach, a deadly combination of last night's spices and the gaseous home brew caused a chemical reaction that sent an explosion of terrifying proportions into the duodenum, forcing a stinking gale both south into the colon and north into the complexities of Liver Central.

'That,' said Ahmed.

'Ugh,' croaked Bill, letting go of Ahmed's sleeve so he could pinch his nose against the strengthening reek.

The Host had farted.

4

Ted Davenport, landlord of The Singing Sphincter, was sweeping up broken glass from the floor of his tavern when Bill and Ahmed entered. The pub was understandably deserted.

'Gentlemen!' The landlord beamed at Ahmed then eyed Bill with more suspicion than welcome. 'What'll ye be having?'

'The usual for me Lord Ted,' said Ahmed cheerfully, using the landlord's popular but completely false moniker. 'This is Bill, the man in charge of Immigration and Foreign... well, IFOO.'

'Bless you,' said Lord Ted with a straight face.

Ahmed, familiar with the joke that was as yet lost on Bill, turned to his old friend. 'Bill, what can I get you to wash away the residues of that embarrassing event?'

'Have you any Madeira?' asked Bill innocently.

Lord Ted guffawed; Ahmed suppressed a chuckle.

'In that case,' muttered Bill, 'a beer please.'

'Gut Wrencher, Padre's Pardon, Liver Purger or Fatima's Flush?' Lord Ted's list of real ales momentarily confused Bill, a reaction that always pleased the landlord because it gave him an opportunity to explain the merits of each.

Ahmed, knowing what would surely follow, was quick to interject. 'Padre's Pardon is a mere 3.8 specific gravity yet delightfully nutty…'

Bill nodded before his chum could go on. 'That'll do me.'

Lord Ted set about pulling two pints of the golden IPA. 'I'm afraid recent events might have unsettled this,' he said. 'Unsettled me and the pub, as it happens.'

'It was a bit, um, explosive,' agreed Ahmed.

'Does that happen often?' asked Bill, taking a sip of the beer that Lord Ted had placed before him. 'Ah, that's welcome, not unsettled at all.'

'Not like that, it doesn't.' Lord Ted had taken the air of The-One-Who-Knows-Everything, as all good landlords do. 'Well, it didn't in the good old days.'

'Good old days?' asked Bill. 'You mean when The Host ate his greens and controlled his passion for curries and home brew?'

'Precisely,' put in Ahmed.

'If you ask me, it's Johnny Foreigner who's put The Host up to this,' said Lord Ted with a frown.

Ahmed, who might have bridled at a reference to foreigners, didn't.

Bill snapped into work mode. 'What do you mean?'

It was Ahmed, who had a more fortunate turn of phrase than his jovial landlord, who explained.

'You know, Bill, that none of us except The Chief can actually influence The Host? Not even you. Here we all are just getting on with our jobs, nose to the grindstone, grist to the mill. Literally. It's what we do. Well, things seem to be changing around here, very subtly.'

'Such as what?' asked Bill, smelling a rat.

'It's difficult to put one's finger on it,' continued Ahmed after a deep draft of Padre's Pardon. 'Normally, hitherto, we all work side by side and everyone in each department knows everyone else, but recently—'

'Recently there have been some shady characters around here.' Lord Ted couldn't help playing the role of Most-Informed-Person-In-the-Community-If-Not-The-Whole-Body.

'Exactly,' said Ahmed, picking up his glass, studying the contents for a moment, then returning it to its resting place on a beer mat boasting the slogan *The Singing Sphincter – established when The Host was still in short trousers*. Next to this someone had scrawled, "Drink up, not much time left".

Bill watched him, carefully. 'Are you saying that there are, well, interlopers in your section, Ahmed?'

'Sadly, yes.'

'Like those characters I came across just before I arrived at your office?'

Ahmed looked at him quizzically. 'Can you describe them?'

'Well, they were a lazy bunch for a start. Fat, greasy, rude. Could barely speak English. Didn't feel comfortable being near them.' Then, in case he had offended a friend with a distinctly foreign name, added: 'I mean, they were ruffians, more akin to reptiles living under a rock than the folk you normally meet in and around Liver Central.'

23

'Exactly,' confirmed Lord Ted. 'Like I said, shady characters.'

'But where did they come from? And why? Are they dangerous?' Bill was beginning to understand that his holiday might be rudely interrupted.

'I have a theory,' said Ahmed, 'but I don't think you're going to like it.'

'Try me,' challenged the Head of IFOO.

'Well, there are growing numbers of these… these interlopers. I didn't appoint them, neither did you, or The Chief. I think they are created by thoughts.'

'Eh?' Bill was incredulous, but the landlord just nodded knowingly as if it was his idea in the first place.

'Yes. Hear me out on this one. It's a new phenomenon.'

'Better have another pint then,' said Bill, pushing his empty glass towards Lord Ted. 'And another to loosen the tongue of my good friend here,' indicating that Ahmed should drink up, 'and one for your good self too.'

Lord Ted obliged.

The theory, if that is what you call putting two and two together, was explained by Ahmed and confirmed by Lord Ted with effusive grunts and interjections, some helpful, others fanciful. But as time went on, and the hour grew late with no more internal or external influences generated by The Host's erratic behaviour of late, and as more of Lord Ted's regulars arrived to whet their whistles, reality dawned on the Head of IFOO.

When Ahmed had finished, Bill said simply: 'Hybrids then? The devil's spawn?'

His blood was up, probably inspired by yet another pint of Padre's Pardon.

'You bet,' agreed Lord Ted as he pulled a pint of Gut Wrencher for one of his regulars.

'Sadly, yes.' Ahmed had his serious face on. 'And I'm not sure what to do about it.'

'Me neither,' said Bill glumly. 'Except for one obvious course of action.'

'Which is?'

'Which is to do what we are trained to do in any circumstances such as these.'

'Go on, as if I didn't know.'

And Bill, a man to whom routine and The Right Thing To Do was second nature, asked his old friend and subordinate, Ahmed, to write a report which he would collect on his return from holiday and present to none other than The Chief herself.

'She'll know what to do.'

Ahmed and Lord Ted raised their glasses.

'We'll drink to that,' they announced in unison.

5

'Bill! You're back, and so soon! Did you have a wonderful time?'

Imelda was quivering in the essential parts not concealed by her latest fashion statement from yesteryear.

Bill grunted what might or might not have been an affirmative and spun Ahmed's report onto The Chief's desk.

'Oh Bill, don't tell me you've been working instead of relaxing? What's this? Surely not one of your *fascinating* reports?'

Bill wasn't sure if there was a note of sarcasm in Imelda's tone but he pushed the thought aside.

'No, Chief, not mine. Ahmed's.'

Imelda picked up the report. It was twenty pages of Univers ten point, single spaced with appropriate sub-divisions, bound with a cheap plastic spine that would not suffer more than half a dozen readers before falling apart. She flicked through it and returned it to her desk, then approached Bill like a galleon in full sail, holding out pink hands towards him in a manner which almost made Bill take a step back.

'Bill, I've missed your calming influence.' She took his hand and tugged him towards the sofa that was reserved for more intimate discussions than those that can be typed in Univers ten point. 'Tell me,' she said in her most husky voice, 'what's this all about?'

Bill positioned himself on what little sofa remained after Imelda had pulled him hard enough to give him no other option.

'Well...' Bill's difficulty in completing sentences resurfaced whenever he was with The Chief.

'Start at the beginning Bill,' insisted Imelda, straightening her floral discovery across an ample lap. 'Never mind Ahmed, tell me about your *holiday*.'

'Well... it wasn't really that much fun. I only got as far as Knee West. I had hoped to go to all the way, but there were no pods that far south and my suit was awful—'

'Bill, you're starting at the end. When you left here you were going to see Nadia about transport arrangements.'

'Ah, Nadia. Yes.'

'Yes?' Imelda snatched back a hand that had been clinging to Bill's. 'Is that all? Just "Yes"?'

'Indeed yes, she arranged everything for a trip via Heart Junction and Liver Central all the way south and asked me to send her a postcard.'

'Hmmm. I'm getting the impression that the crux of your short break all happened in a conversation with Nadia. If not that, at Liver Central. Am I right?'

Bill nodded slowly, hoping this was the moment of his escape from a confession that, as holidays go, he hadn't really had one, and by not having one at his age, would probably never succeed in discovering what all the fuss was about.

'That's why I've brought you Ahmed's report,' he said. 'Things are pretty bad down there.'

'Bad? In what way?'

'Well...'

'Oh Bill, *do* stop saying "well" all the time.'

'Sorry. Well, there seem to be a large number of, er, unwelcome types in the general area of The Host's liver.'

Imelda stiffened. 'Not flukes?'

Bill shook his head violently. 'No, no. Not flukes. At least none that I've seen, or Ahmed for that matter, thank God.'

'What then?'

'Worse than flukes. To all intents and purposes they are just like us, only they're not... not *nice*.'

'Who are they, then?'

'Well, Ahmed thinks they are created by, ah, by *thoughts*, a kind of figment of The Host's imagination, but definitely made of flesh and blood just like you and me.'

'You and *I*.'

'Pardon?'

'Never mind. Go on.'

'Well, Ahmed has this theory – it's all in the report – that The Host has lost touch with the old ways of homely living, and the more he lets himself go, the more he opens up his body to all sorts of foreign invaders.'

Imelda put her hand to her mouth with a sharp intake of breath. 'You mean…'

'Well, yes. I mean he has allowed this lackadaisical attitude to have free reign, and when a human has a lackadaisical approach, we all know that all manner of things can go horribly wrong. I've seen it with my own eyes. There are people – things – down there who are definitely not doing their best for The Host. Quite the opposite.'

'What are they then?'

'Let's just call them the enemy. Worse than flukes. We can get rid of flukes with a bit of courage and a firm hand. But these… they are something else.'

'Oh my. Bill, what are we going to do?'

Bill had never seen Imelda so disturbed. Normally she was assured. He put his arm around her, allowing his fingers to rest on a broad expanse of shoulder.

'We're going to find a way.' He felt like a man, though he had no idea what that way would be.

'Good. Good.' Suddenly The Chief was on her feet. She picked up Ahmed's report and leafed through it again, not seeing the words but feeling the strength that Bill's words had given her. 'Good, good, *good.* Bill, I'm putting you in charge of this whole operation, and when we've found a way to deal with this crisis, you are going to have a proper holiday. I want a meeting tomorrow, early, of all divisional heads. And that includes Ahmed.'

'Chief? Is that wise? Surely we need Ahmed keeping an eye on things down there?'

'Could they get any worse? If what you are telling me is true we have a crisis here to surpass any peanut choking, a bad case of mumps, even the clap. This is serious Bill and you know it. What goes wrong down at Liver Central affects us all. Get it wrong there and we're all out of a job.'

Bill looked at his feet and longed for his pipe with a full bowl of Mother Nag tobacco and a pint of Padre's Pardon. At this point he could have decided to retire, but with a surge of what others might call adrenalin, or true grit, or stiff upper lip, he pulled himself together.

He lifted his manly chin and looked The Chief in the eye.

'I'm on to it,' he said.

'Go to it,' she replied.

Bill turned to leave but Imelda reached out a hand to touch him on the shoulder.

'You were always the right man for a crisis.' Her eyes were dewy.

'But we haven't had a crisis like this before,' he replied firmly.

'Looks like we have now,' she said and turned back to Ahmed's report.

6

The Boardroom was only used for emergencies and annual meetings. As The Host rarely presented any health problems that might be construed as an emergency, it was only ever occupied in earnest on the last Friday before Christmas when Imelda dispensed decanted sweet sherry and mince pies.

It was also used by Junior Brain Maintenance Officer Gerry Hadwell for secret trysts with the office cleaner, Wendy, who was attractive in a quirky kind of way and old enough to be Gerry's mother. And as it was nowhere near Christmastime, the lovers had no idea that their secret was in imminent danger of being discovered by none other than The Chief herself.

A good thing, then, that when Imelda entered humming *The White Cliffs of Dover* she was carrying a pile of reference books that included all three volumes of *Entwhistle's Encyclopaedia of Nutrition* and *The Psychology of Human Relationships*, and that neither Gerry nor Wendy had as yet removed any clothing apart from Gerry's old school tie.

Unable to deploy either hand to push open the door, Imelda had used her well-padded rear portion to achieve this objective. She couldn't see through *The Psychology of Human Relationships*, which runs to 837 pages including forewords by several eminent professors of the last century, so she was unaware that there was anyone else in the Boardroom as she entered.

Wendy was not as dumb as her bleach blonde hair would suggest. Understanding the crisis with lightning speed, she indicated with her eyes that Gerry should tiptoe through the open door as fast as he could before The Chief either put down the books or dropped them. As he left, breathing in as he passed just inches from Imelda's hind quarters, crabbing sideways, Wendy pulled a duster from her shirt pocket – she always kept a duster there whether working or off duty – and proceeded to polish the Boardroom table. Or at least give that impression.

Imelda allowed the books to tumble onto the table and, noticing Wendy with a start, exclaimed: 'Wendy! What are you doing here?'

With barely a pause in her industrious dusting, Wendy replied: 'Ma'am, I always try to keep things in readiness.'

'Oh you little poppet,' beamed Imelda, 'we've got a very important crisis meeting in five minutes. Hurry up, get yourself off home, and maybe tomorrow clear up after us all.'

'Yes. Of course Ma'am.' If she hadn't been dusting she might have curtsied. She felt flustered and relieved at the same time. Imelda didn't notice the flush of pink at her cleavage nor the telltale flutter of eyelashes heavy with overdone mascara.

'Off you go then. They'll be arriving soon.'

'Who, Ma'am?'

'The Cabinet of course. Got to keep this ship on course, don't you know?'

This made Wendy feel extremely important, so she obeyed, tucking her duster into her shirt pocket and side-footing Gerry's discarded tie behind a bookcase as she left.

Imelda resumed her humming, in her mind the bit about the bluebirds.

'... I was saying only yesterday how *fortunate* we've been. Everything running like clockwork. No alarms as far back as I can recall...'

The speaker was Digby, Head of New and Interesting Technology, NIT for short. He had an arm around Bill's shoulders and his bushy eyebrows were almost within touching distance of the IFOO director's nose. Though bloodshot from one too many pink gins at lunch, his eyes retained that most appealing characteristic, laughter. His silver hair showered dandruff not just on his own navy blue blazer, but also on Bill's ageing tweed.

'... Ah, Imelda my dear, how lovely you look. Always a pleasure...'

Digby released his arm from Bill's shoulders to lurch towards Imelda who visibly braced herself for a ritual triple kiss in the continental style, not to mention some naughty touching and squeezing favoured by the Head of NIT. Bill took his opportunity to circumvent the Boardroom table to take a seat that he hoped would leave several square metres of solid oak between himself and his overbearing colleague.

'Digby,' Imelda gasped after being released from the resulting grope, 'you're looking very dapper today.'

She was saved from an exposition of the latest men's fashion, which it has to be said did not suit the inelegant Digby one jot, by the arrival of Isabella of Special Cardiac and Blood Systems (SCABS), beautifully arrayed in a blinding Flamenco dress slit to the thigh and set off by a plastic red rose nestling in her abundant black hair.

She was so spectacular that only Bill noticed Ahmed slide into the room and, spotting that Bill was the only one seated, the LADS foreman eased himself gratefully into the chair next to him.

'Ah,' said Imelda firmly, 'we have a quorum. Let's get started shall we?' Digby and Isabella took their seats opposite Ahmed and Bill as Imelda forced herself into a slightly larger – and wider – chair at the head of the table. 'Ahmed, it is your report that has brought us all together…?'

'Yes Ma'am,' replied Ahmed, for whom the seriousness of the situation had somehow subdued his usual cockiness. 'Yes Indeedy' or 'You Betcha' would have been his expected response.

He outlined his report in about ten minutes of passionate explanation leaving no one in any doubt that there was indeed a serious situation and that there was no precedent for dealing with a problem like this.

'Round 'em all up, line 'em up against a fibia or a tibia, and shoot them. That's what I say.'

The others looked at Digby with a combination of shock and horror.

'Digby, really!' said Imelda with a Chairwoman's authority. 'There are correct ways of dealing with this.'

Bill took his opportunity to contribute. 'Perhaps Digby's approach isn't so far-fetched? I mean, what we have here is an unprecedented undercover attack on The Host which is, may I remind you, a direct attack on each and every one of us.'

'And what do we shoot them with? Lentils and dried peas?' Isabella's sensual accent had a calming effect.

Ahmed decided to elaborate on his findings.

'There is something more,' he said solemnly. 'We have found a nest of cancer cells.'

The effect was astounding. A full thirty seconds of complete silence.

'I beg your pardon?' said Imelda, eventually. 'Did you say *cancer cells*?'

'Why didn't you tell me this before?' Bill whispered to his old friend. Everyone heard.

'Because we only discovered it after you left,' Ahmed whispered back through gritted teeth.

'Cancer? Cancer?' screeched Isabella as she stood and thumped the table. 'Don't you realise that I'll have to go immediately to red alert? It's my system that's going to carry these... these *enemies* all around The Host. We're all going to die!'

She would have continued her outburst but Imelda, behaving exactly as The Chief should, also rose to her feet and commanded firmly: 'Enough, Isabella!'

Isabella sat and looked as though she might cry.

'Bill,' said Imelda more gently when calm had resumed, 'this is your area. What do you suggest?'

Bill cleared his throat. He had never seen a cancer cell and had never researched their effect on a human. It had never crossed his mind to do so because he believed with all his heart that The Host, Brian Davis of The Poplars, Watford, was leading a charmed life and would live to a ripe old age without any of the encumbrances so often seen in western society. The Host was "in the pink" as far as Bill was concerned and long may he remain so.

'I've heard it said,' he began slowly, 'that if your host has one cancer cell, there will soon be millions. I want you all to know that I don't believe this. To be sure, we are under attack like never before, but before we go around shooting aliens with lentils and peas, I think we should ask Ahmed for more information.' Turning to his friend, he added: 'What do *you* think we should do?'

Always a good Boardroom policy to pass the buck.

To Bill's relief, Ahmed had an answer.

'These few cells were outside the liver, thankfully, in the entrance to the bowel. I immediately had them hosed with freshly digested cucumber that had come down mixed with mayonnaise, indigestible processed beef and a ton or three of white bread. I think humans call it a bun, or a bap or something, whatever, I call it *crap*. It was so sugar-rich we had to wash it first. But what we really need is something with a heck of a lot of vitamin C in it. Otherwise we're sunk.'

Isabella was straight back on her feet. 'Vitamin C? Where in the Sweet Holy Name are we going to get *that* from?'

'Patience, Isabella.' The Chief was coming into her own, though she also passed the buck. Back to Ahmed.

'Any ideas, Ahmed?'

Ahmed shrugged his shoulders.

And Bill made the first mistake of his distinguished career with IFOO. He had an answer, and volunteered it without thinking of the consequences. This was the golden rule that if you make a suggestion you sure as hell are going to be saddled with getting off your backside and doing it yourself.

'It has to come from Mrs Host,' he said. 'From his wife. Betty, I think her name is, if I'm not mistaken?'

7

The Plan was audacious. Not in the training manuals. And not viable as far as Bill was concerned.

Who in their right mind would take their life in their hands by actually exiting The Host and going to beg favour of another human being's Protectorate?

Unheard of.

And downright stupid if you ask me, thought Bill.

But he agreed in his own personal whirlpool of stupidity because his upper lip remained stiff and he had always secretly wanted to be a hero.

As to The Big Plan to get Bill out of The Host and into close proximity with the Betty Davis Protectorate Staff, there lay a problem for which every member of the cabinet had a solution – except Bill.

Digby's idea was to suit up Bill and shove him forcefully through The Host's anus, an idea that Bill suspected was borne out of some schoolboy mischief to do with "taking a dump".

Isabella wondered, quaintly, if The Host could not be induced to sneeze Bill out of the body while taking in the sweet aromas of a rose bush in the garden.

39

Both Ahmed and Bill sat silently, despondently, with their heads in their hands.

It was The Chief who came up with the simplest and safest form of exit. She was beginning to explain her idea when there was a frantic knocking on the Boardroom door.

'What the—' Ahmed began.

Bill hoped that whatever the disturbance, it would get everyone's mind off this appalling idea.

'Come in,' called Imelda.

The oak door squeaked slowly open and a head peeped around it. It was Gerry, blushing like a tomato and tie-less.

'Excuse me,' began Gerry timorously, 'but I couldn't help noticing…'

'Notice what? Get on with it man,' boomed Digby, ever the bully.

'Gerry, come in, and tell us what this is all about,' said Imelda calmly.

Gerry obeyed. He stood like a schoolboy who has been caught smoking behind the bike sheds, head bowed, hands behind his back, and explained.

'Well, Ma'am, I was passing your office—'

Digby pounced. "Poking your snotty little nose where you shouldn't, I don't doubt!'

'Digby, please!' said Imelda, 'let the man speak. It might be important. Gerry, you were passing my office?'

'Yes,' said Gerry meekly, 'and I noticed that your lights were flashing.'

'Lights? The red ones?' asked Imelda, slightly alarmed.

'Yes the red ones. So I went in. The door wasn't locked.'

'Or you picked it...' Digby was being more annoying than usual.

'Digby, I shan't tell you again! Go on, Gerry. Which lights?'

'The ones labelled "Testosterone Alert".'

To a man, or a woman in the case of The Chief and the Head of SCABS, all closed their eyes with a collective, "Oh No!".

And then, in unison, held on to the table.

'He can't,' said Isabella.

'He definitely can't,' muttered Bill.

'He bloody well can,' said Digby and dived under the table as the room began to rock.

A good five years had passed since any of them had experienced anything like it. Furniture slid, pictures crashed to the floor, the bookcase concealing Gerry's tie slid a full five metres sideways and back again, and the chandelier swayed and tinkled as if it were an orchestra in its own right.

Gerry, the only one not clinging to the table, rolled and slid with the bookcase.

At one stage Bill found himself in close proximity with The Chief's bottom but he was suddenly dragged back the way he had come and saved himself further ignominy by grasping an oak table leg. From his new position he thought he saw

Digby with his head beneath Isabella's skirts, but didn't have time to weigh up his observation as the room seemed to turn turtle.

Calm resumed after what seemed an age of tumbling and sliding. The moans and groans could have been uttered by The Cabinet members, or then again they could have been an echo from an alien world. At least alien these past five years.

All were panting in that moment of relief after The Catastrophe, except Isabella who was not to be seen. Or Digby.

Imelda, as The Chief should, was first to recover.

'Now where were we?' she asked, gathering up three volumes of *Entwhistle's Encyclopaedia of Nutrition* and *The Psychology of Human Relationships*, re-stacking them in some semblance of order on the Boardroom table.

'We were in heaven, I think,' said a dishevelled Isabella, poking her head above the table. Her hair was awry and the rose had disappeared.

Bill, who felt distinctly unwell, watched the chandelier swaying. Ahmed smirked. Digby reappeared.

'As I said,' Imelda said sternly, 'where were we?'

'I think you were hatching a plan to restore natural order to The Host's latest, ah, medical problem?'

'Indeed I was,' said Imelda, flushing.

'Well then,' said Bill, proud to be displaying little emotion in what was undoubtedly an emotional experience for them all, 'remind me of your plan.'

When you are faced with a suicide mission, you discover a new resourcefulness. It's like going into to bat in a cricket match with snarling, hairy fast bowler pacing out the longest run-up you've ever seen. Or being a four-foot first receiver with three enormous hulks bearing down upon you, evil eyes flashing and nostrils flaring.

Bill's head felt heavy on his load-bearing hands as Imelda outlined the objectives of his mission.

'You must link up as quickly as possible with your oppo,' she said with a breathy voice that only added to the sense of excitement around the table, 'and of course the first thing you must do is identify yourself carefully so that their Head of IFOO–'

'Bless you,' said Digby.

'–so that their head of *Foreign Objects* doesn't mistake you for an unwelcome insect or something and call in the heavies.'

'An insect?' protested Bill.

Ahmed sniggered.

Digby retorted: 'Looks like a cockroach, doesn't he?'

'Floats like a butterfly, stings like a bee,' was Isabella's aside.

'Enough!' Imelda thumped the table. 'We're asking Bill to go out on a limb here—'

'Literally.' Digby was now annoying everyone.

'—and if you don't button it, Digby, it will be you braving the unknown, though in your case I think the word "braving" to be off the mark.'

Bill brought the meeting back to order. 'Do I deliver a verbal or a written message?'

'I think you know the form, Bill, you of all people know the implications of Ahmed's discovery. And I trust you implicitly to work with the other team to find a solution.'

'Best case scenario?' Unusual terminology for Bill, but he was under immense pressure.

Imelda took a deep breath and did what all good Chiefs would do in a crisis. She provided a list.

'One, that their team understands the danger of what's going on over here. Two, that they understand what's causing that danger. Three, to ascertain if they have a solution to our problem and four, a plan to implement it. Understood?'

'Yes, Ma'am,' said Bill obediently.

'You'll need some equipment, not least a decent travel suit.'

'Of course. Preferably one that doesn't make me look like an alien invader,' said Bill laconically. 'Where from?'

'Outer space?' Digby again. But this time with a *soupçon* less sarcasm.

Imelda ignored him. 'Nadia will have what you need in her stores. I'll write you a chitty.'

Bill's day had suddenly brightened.

8

The map was confusing. It appeared to show a labyrinth of tunnels and caves. With Imelda's and Ahmed's help, Bill had used a marker pen to trace his route.

But no amount of planning had prepared Bill for the terrible sounds of the Inner Ear.

His suit was merely an under garment. Needing more pockets for maps, torch, water bottle, scissors, string, sticking plasters, hanky, a hip flask and a packet of digestives, Bill had pulled on a pair of many-pocketed combat trousers lent to him by Ahmed and a pink puffa jacket, courtesy of Nadia. The hood of his suit contained a complex radio system and a hands-free microphone that wobbled somewhere near the corner of his mouth. Nadia had also supplied him with light-enhancing goggles that made him look like a steampunk with a perversion, tufts of grey hair forced outwards by the elasti-cised strap around his head. Across his shoulders was a coiled rope and at his belt hung two large hooks with which, Ahmed had theorised, he could extricate himself from a life-time's confinement within The Host.

But the noise bordered on unbearable. It was like being si-multaneously in the middle of a tornado and a terrorist at-tack. The roaring and crashing sounds were amplified by a wind that blew strongly then sucked like a vacuum cleaner without any warning of a change in direction, all the time accompanied by the pounding of what seemed to be a huge kettle drum.

'Come in, Bill, report please. Over.' Imelda's voice crackled in his ear, barely competing with the extraneous sounds.

'I'm entering the perilymph now,' Bill shouted, his voice so distorted that both Imelda and Ahmed thought they heard *'I'm entering a comely nymph now'* and looked at each other in temporary confusion.

'Dirty old man,' said Ahmed and instantly regretted it.

'Perilymph or endolymph?' asked The Chief in the comfort of her office.

'End of *what?*' asked an incredulous Bill.

'Which part of the inner ear?' screeched Imelda.

'Dunno, it's a very wet lymph…'

Ahmed suppressed a smile as the link died leaving him with the impression of Bill encountering a very wet nymph.

'I think he's moving towards the ear drum,' he said. 'Even if the radio was working, it must be deafening for him and would probably break our speakers.'

'Oh dear,' said Imelda, 'we can't have that, can we? We'll just have to hope that he can manage without us. Will he be able to reach us once he's past the ear drum?'

Ahmed shrugged. 'Don't know,' he admitted, 'he's boldly going into the unknown…'

'I do hope he'll be all right. I mean, it's so worrisome.'

'Don't you worry about Bill,' replied Ahmed, 'after all, he's got his suicide pills.'

'Suicide pills?'

'Only kidding,' said Ahmed laconically, 'Bill's our man, he won't let us down.'

What Ahmed didn't know was that Bill felt extremely suicidal as he hoisted himself over the stirrup and tried to propel himself towards The Host's eardrum. Because he needed both hands to make this precarious manoeuvre, he was unable to block his ears. He knew The Host was snoring – that wasn't hard for a man of his advanced years to deduce – but the sheer volume combined with the unearthly movement of air, the *physical* vibration caused by the pulsating eardrum beyond, was almost too much to bear.

He held the thinnest part of the stirrup bone with his legs in a scissor grip, pulled out the handkerchief and, after tearing it in two, stuffed each part into his ears. This only partially muffled the thunderous noise, but it made him feel slightly less suicidal.

He watched the quivering eardrum below, loosened the grip of his legs, and for a moment hung precariously above the taught, vibrating membrane.

He prayed.

And let go.

His landing coincided with The Host's in-breath and the resulting sound wave shot him upwards again so that he resembled a somersaulting insect, propelled without control or grace to the roof of the Eustachian tube, and thence back towards the offending eardrum. But this time he landed in a soft mucous to one side of the sonorous organ.

To his relief, the noise was less deafening in the sticky goo that had cushioned his fall, though this presented a further obstacle to his mission. Finding yourself in a squelchy mess is only marginally better than being hurled out of control by a thunderous eardrum. Disorientated, he hauled himself in what he hoped was the right direction.

The external auditory canal is heaven compared to being bounced around between the eardrum and the squishy Eustachian tube. Bill made a mental note to suggest this latter as a holiday destination to the thrill-seeking junior members of IFOO. Thrill-a-minute EustaLand. Better than playing hide-and-seek within The Host's nasal hair.

He pulled himself together, adjusted his goggles, wiped as much mucous from his puffa jacket as he could, and jutted his courageous jaw towards an eerie glow beyond.

The great Otherworld of humans and myths.

The Host's earwax presented only minor problems.

Though his adventurer's boots tended to stick in it, and only come free with a gloopy sucking sound, he made steady progress towards the light. The wind was slight here, and the booming noises grew marginally fainter. He fiddled with the knobs on his light-enhancing goggles, which made no difference at all, and concentrating on the light ahead made the sort of steady progress he had always admired in the biographies of Great Adventurers in *Massey's Olde Almanacke Of Greate Adventures*.

But he had not prepared himself for the monster that sat in the exit so warmly recommended to him by the Cabinet.

As he adjusted his eyes to the shimmering light, an enormous shadow loomed before him. He peered at it, heart pounding. It had bulbous eyes, scaly black skin, and very

48

long legs, its snout seemingly longer still. What it was doing with its snout offended Bill. It was thrust into the pink fleshy part of the exit chosen for him and was pulsing with the crimson life-blood that all his colleagues at IFOO, LADS and especially SCABS cherished almost beyond life itself.

It was *drinking* The Host's *blood*.

He gathered himself.

And charged.

It is difficult to charge when wax clings to your feet, but charge he did. In slow motion.

One of the bulbous eyes swivelled lazily and fixed him with a stare.

Bill leapt.

'Oh no you don't!' he screamed as he attempted to fly through the air, imagining the shock and awe as his bony frame collided with that obnoxious snout.

But his left foot remained ensnared in wax and he fell clumsily to the floor of the external auditory canal.

The creature's other eye swivelled and both now fixed him with a stare.

Bill reached into one of his many pockets and pulled out his hip flask. He flung it at the monster, hitting it in one of those ghastly eyes.

With a whir of silvery wings, the creature detached its disgusting snout, dripping blood, and fled.

Bill crawled towards the fallen but victorious flask. He had filled it with *Gold Cask Seven Star* last night in anticipation of its undoubted restorative properties, but never in his wildest dreams had he thought he might defeat a blood-sucking dragon with it.

He unscrewed the silver stopper, took a slug, and looked out into the world of humans.

9

If Bill had ever looked over a cliff before, the giddiness and nausea might have been familiar. He wanted to return to the waxy safety inside The Host's ear despite its jungle of massive hairs and the incessant booming noise, yet he was inexorably drawn to the edge of the lobe and the breathtaking scene beyond, enhanced by his goggles.

A silvery light played over a vast plain some distance below. The terrain appeared to subtly change colour with hues of deep blue and shadowy greys. The sounds were fainter here, The Host's breathing rolling like distant thunder, lost in the vastness of this human world.

There was no sign of the dragon.

Bill peered into the mysterious gloom and made out the darker shape of what looked like a mountain range beyond the plain, the nearest mound crowned with whorls of growth that seemed to entwine a dozen huge cylindrical shapes like spiky logs. The giant creature – he knew it must be Mrs Host – was also emitting strange grumbling sounds, more rhythmic and gentler than those of his own world.

He watched this alien scene, taking in its richness, it's sheer *volume*, his hands clutching the edge of a precipice, not caring nor thinking about moving. Yet he did not feel alarmed. He just wondered if he would be able to find the words to describe it to Imelda and Ahmed. Digby, of course, would not be interested, at least as long as Isabella was nearby. But he, the Head of IFOO, was privileged to look out upon a world of vastness and endless possibilities. So much to explore and try to understand.

Yet so fraught with unknown dangers.

He took a deep breath and willed himself to continue with his mission.

He took a hook from his belt, attached one end of the rope and secured it around a particularly stout hair that grew fully to thrice his own height. He dropped the rope over the precipice and peered after it, clutching the ridge as best he could with one hand. It was not clear whether the rope reached the bottom of the cliff but he could see it had come to rest among some longer strands of silvery hair somewhere near the cliff's base. Something to offer a firm grip, he hoped.

But Bill was a virgin adventurer, never having had need of a long rope in his lifetime. Somehow he managed to slip and slide to a point somewhere near his objective before his fingers lost their grip and he fell, tumbling in a most ungainly display through the tangled hairs of The Host, landing on what turned out to be a pleasantly soft surface. He was unhurt. He passed a hand over the surface, marvelling at its silky sheen.

He lingered too long, unaware of the danger he faced. For Brian Davis of The Poplars, Watford, senior partner at Grimson, Ramsbotham and Davis, chartered accountants, chose that moment of Bill's wonderment at the surface of a pillowcase costing £3.95 from Littlewoods to have a disturbing dream and, in an attempt to dispel its horrors, turned over in his sleep.

Bill was sent flying by a thick strand of human hair as the cliff face down which he had descended suddenly rose up, creating a swirling wind like a typhoon and a mass of hairs, each with a circumference many times that of Bill's waist, brittle and therefore hard, whipped menacingly in all directions. The savage blow from that particular hair saved his life. He landed further along the silky plain just as an enormous nose the size of a mountain crashed down on the very spot where he had been.

He bounced. Fortunately further away from The Host's head. Thick strands of hair, like giant Gorgonesque snakes, showered him with heavy white flakes of dead body cells. They stank. But Bill was safe.

For now.

He stared in horror at the scene. The huge nose that had almost claimed his life was bent at what would have been a comical angle if it hadn't been for the gale it now emitted, blasting Bill yet further away along the plain. The smell was appalling. Spicy but stale. With the image of those hair-lined nostrils and a huge, cavernous mouth in his mind, Bill did what any self-respecting adventurer would do.

He ran.

Or rather slipped and slid on the alien plain as fast as he could stagger.

So intent was he on watching for further dangers, mostly on his back with his bony legs pushing for all they were worth, that he was unaware of the speed with which he crossed the plain. So when his shoulders pushed against something solid, he stopped his frantic struggle for life, and braced himself for his next nightmare. He reached one hand behind him. He touched something slimy.

Slowly, he turned his head.

His hand was resting on a film of liquid that covered an expanse of translucent membrane. It vibrated to his touch. He thought it looked mostly white yet it was filled with a rainbow of colours reflecting the eerie light. Above it and below a row of ordered dark hairs quivered, each so thick at their base it would take himself, Ahmed and The Chief linking hands to reach around it.

Bill felt as though he was being watched.

He extended a finger and poked the membrane. Tiny ripples extended outwards from his touch. The pool darkened but in the centre of the disturbance a tiny light shone, then gradually grew brighter and wider. He put his goggled face as close as he dared.

And there, shimmering behind the strange surface like some kind of water sprite, he saw a face.

It was a beautiful face, with tangled golden hair and eyes like aquamarines.

And those startling eyes were watching him.

10

Bill had been outside of The Host for too long but he didn't care. Those parts of his skin that were exposed to dry air and unknown bacteria, namely his face and his hands, were beginning to react to the alien environment. His skin felt brittle. It was painful. But the woman he was watching soothed that discomfort to the point where he barely noticed it.

Her large round eyes were definitely smiling at him.

He tried to smile back but the combination of the taught goggles and the condition of his skin made this difficult so instead he waved tentatively. She waved back, then put her hand to her mouth as if contemplating an unusual predicament in which the only means of communication was a series of shy waves and unilateral smiles. She pointed downwards.

Bill instinctively checked that his flies were not undone.

With an amused look on her face, the golden woman pointed again and Bill understood. He was to climb upon a human's lower eyelid and ease himself into the conjunctiva and thence gain access through the aqueous fluid at the corner of the eye. That would feel more like home, he thought, as long as this beautiful creature's Host did not blink. (He had not even begun to wonder why a human would sleep with eye or eyes open but that did not concern him when confronted by such a delightful apparition).

He moved towards the corner as instructed, then stopped. Maybe he should try to report in? He clicked the radio's "on" switch and sent a terse message.

'Have encountered beautiful nymph-like creature. Believe subject is Host Protector. Am going in. Over.'

There was a strange hissing sound but no reply so he repeated his message, then with a shrug intended to give the impression that he was a courageous professional who did not need to rely on technology, eased himself into the conjunctiva's mucous.

Even through his combats, puffa jacket, skin suit and adventurer's boots, it was warm and welcoming. He filled his lungs with it and felt instantly better while his skin, with restored elasticity, at last stopped stinging. He emerged into the vitreous cavity where the angel swam towards him and took his hand, tugging him towards a hatch that he guessed would open into the hyaloid canal where the going would be easier.

It was. Not just easier to stand and walk, but also to talk.

She didn't let go of his hand.

Bill gaped.

She giggled.

'Why don't you take those silly things off your face? You look like a... well, a goggle-eyed thing,' she smiled.

He had forgotten he was wearing them and snatched the goggles hurriedly from his head, stuffing them into his largest pocket.

'I... er... well...' he stammered.

'Your name is Erwell?'

'No, no, no. My name is Bill. What's yours?'

'Angelique.'

Angelique, Angel, Angelic, Bill was thinking. *Angelicious, Heavenly Creature, Angel...* he suddenly realised he was staring at her, making her feel uncomfortable, and cursed himself for his rudeness.

'I'm sorry,' he said at last, 'I have come from your Host's husband, Brian Davis of–'

'I know,' she said quickly. 'About time too. We have been worried.'

'But how did you know I was coming?'

She let go of his hand and tapped the side of her nose with her finger. 'All will be explained. You'd better come with me. The Mother welcomes you.'

'Your mother?'

'Yes, The Mother. Do you not have one over there?'

Bill was thoughtful for a moment, then the light dawned. 'We have The Chief. Imelda. She's a kind of mother I suppose.'

'You call your Mother a chief?' Her eyes widened. 'Like a tribal warlord, or an engineer? What is this chief like?'

Bill said the thing that immediately sprung to mind. 'She has beautiful thoughts.'

'Then she is *A Mother*,' Angelique emphasised, and took his hand again. 'Come on...'

* * *

57

Being inside Betty Davis of The Poplars, Watford, mother and grandmother, housewife and sometime charity worker, was completely different from the world of IFOO.

For start, the passageways were spotlessly clean and decorated here and there with multi-coloured ribbons. It smelled nice, too, like flowers and incense. There seemed to be music, a floaty sound that was always coming from around the next corner though Bill was uncertain whether it was inside his head or Betty's.

And animals. Not like the stray cat with which he shared an office, but creatures that were as exotic as Angelique herself: brightly coloured birds with trailing tails, squat-legged fluff balls that bounced and rolled instead of walking, and pink cats that talked. Well, Bill was convinced they spoke to Angelique and she to them, though he could not understand the language.

But they didn't talk as much as his guide.

'We're going to use the airway,' she was saying as Bill watched a giant moth with blue and purple wings flutter towards them. 'It's such fun, especially at night when the biorhythms are best.'

'Biorhythms...?'

'Oh, I'm sorry, don't you have those? No? Ah well, you'll see. They come from the Moon and take you where you are thinking. You tune into them. Easy peasy...'

Bill was unfamiliar with the term *easy peasy*. She'll start saying "Like" all the time and wanting to play tag or Blind Man's Bluff, he thought. Yet he warmed to her youthful, even childish mannerisms and speech and felt a lot younger than he did when he had left his Host.

A mouse with spectacles and a walking stick doffed his hat to Angelique and then eyed him suspiciously. He had been about to ask for the anatomical co-ordinates of the "airway" and the source of "biorhythms" but the sight he had just witnessed made him feel quite unwell.

'…and then we'll show you our Mansion of Love…'

Bill had not been listening but that restored his attention.

'Mansion of *Love?* What on earth–'

'Why, our Host's brain, where we see and listen. The centre of our being.'

Bill stopped in his tracks and turned Angelique toward him with a hand on her shoulder.

'Do you have a boardroom then?'

'A *boardroom*? What's that?'

'It's a big room with a big table and chairs all round it where decisions are made. Like we have over there...' he waved a hand in the vague direction of where his Host might be '…in our Host, where The Chief holds meetings when important things crop up.'

'Oh no, we don't need a boardroom,' beamed Angelique who turned and skipped ahead. Bill forced his inadequate legs to chase after her and was soon out of breath. He felt hot and uncomfortable under his ridiculous puffa jacket.

He was about to summon extra speed when his guide suddenly disappeared. One minute she was skipping ahead, Bill panting in his effort to keep up, the next she leapt into the air with an excited '*Woo-hoo*' and plunged into what might as well have been an abyss.

Bill couldn't stop. It takes effort to get legs like his to behave in a rapid forward motion pattern, but even more energy to stop them once they have begun. He told them to stop, he told his brain to cease feeding him nonsense about rats with hats and canes, of talking cats and psychedelic butterflies.

His legs disobeyed and his brain could not respond at all.

The Head of IFOO plunged into the respiratory tract with as much dignity as a vicar on six pints of Padre's Pardon of a Sunday afternoon after delivering a matins sermon on the sins of alcohol excess.

11

Angelique bounced. So did Bill.

But not on anything solid.

One minute he was plummeting down in a most ungainly manner but before he hit the ground he was suddenly hurled upwards again by a powerful up draught. It was terrifying and at the same time exhilarating. As frightening as his one and only prostate inspection when the Host reached forty, yet more exciting than anything he had ever experienced before.

Angelique flew past him. Travelling upwards. Perhaps his puffa jacket and over-stuffed pockets were causing too much drag. She fluttered and giggled while he turned somersaults and grunted, his brain in overdrive with calculations about wind speed, his weight, his inappropriate clothing and the likely source of the wind which suddenly reversed again and he dropped like a stone.

When he landed he was more disorientated than he had been on several pints in Lord Ted's pub.

A fairy landed on his nose. It was too close to focus upon, but it was definitely a fairy. A blur of wings and colours, making a sound like trickling water. Angelique was sitting cross-legged next to him.

'Are we up or down?' he asked, involuntarily swatting the fairy aside.

'Very up,' she replied. 'And leave the love bug alone, it only wants to welcome you.'

'Welcome me where?' Bill rummaged in his pockets for the hip flask containing the precious *Gold Cask Seven Star*. He unscrewed the top and tipped it to his mouth. Looking around he saw more light than his tired old eyes were used to and the music had changed to a single chord that somehow made him feel quite calm despite his recent exertions.

'Mansion One,' she said, 'what you would call the frontal lobe.'

'Ah.'

Bill's work rarely took him to his Host's frontal lobe, but he had studied its functions along with every part of the human body system. He watched what looked like a dust devil skittering across a purple floor before exploding in a mass of colours, sending bright flowers in all directions. Detached petals landed softly around them.

'She's dreaming. There are always flowers in her dreams.'

'You can see her dreams?' Bill was incredulous. He never indulged in the passive thoughts of his own Host mainly because they were always dark and brooding.

'Of course. Can't you?'

'Wouldn't want to.'

'Why not? It's such a fun thing to do.'

'What's a fun thing?'

Angelique reached out a hand and he took it.

'Come,' she said. 'I'll show you.'

Bill obeyed, and so did his legs. He allowed her to pull him towards the mass of floating flowers. She reached out with the hand that wasn't clutching Bill's and touched a large, deep red peony. It suddenly multiplied into a dozen more flowers and the chord swelled, changing from a minor to a major.

Bill tried to do the same. He touched a floating flower.

The chord went back to a minor.

'Hmm,' said Angelique, suddenly letting go of his hand. 'You've got a lot to learn. Don't touch anything until after your cleansing. We don't want any nightmares here.'

'Cleansing? Nightmares?'

'Yes. I think you have brought too much negativity with you.'

'Negative? Moi? I'll have you know that without me the Host would have been banged up or homeless years ago!'

Deep down, Bill wanted this delightful creature to fall at his feet in admiration. After all, he was so much older than her and more experienced to boot; there was *nothing* he didn't know about blood cells, antibodies, good and bad bacteria and general well-being. But somewhere deep down he felt inferior, as if he had let all his knowledge and his intense pursuit of unwelcome invaders deflect him from the paramount ideal of a healthy host thinking positive thoughts.

He felt dirty next to this deliciously flighty young thing.

He ought, perhaps, to change his ways. Maybe even take her back to meet the Chief? On second thoughts that might upset the apple cart when all that was needed was a step back to the good old days when nothing could harm their Host.

Angelique seemed to sense Bill's inner turmoil.

'Come along,' she said gaily, taking his hand again. 'Time to meet the others.'

'Righty ho,' said Bill, telling his legs to follow the cutest little bottom he had ever seen.

Yes, he was most certainly getting younger.

Angelique, who seemed to *run* everywhere, actually slowed to a walk as she approached what appeared to be an enormous archway made of sparkling diamonds. She let go of Bill's hand and advanced towards it, arms outstretched as if absorbing the very essence of the light.

Bill was awed but managed to follow her across a threshold that itself had no substance, just a reflection of the dazzling aura around them. He had reached the stage where nothing would surprise him anymore and trusted the mysterious ground to support him. Which, to his amazement, it did.

Angelique went ahead, her hands now held before her in a recognisable form of ritualistic supplication. Beyond her the light was so dazzling it was several moments – and tentative steps – before he realised there were other beings watching his approach. At first he could only see their eyes, lights within the light, watching with sparkling enthusiasm tinged with surprise and, perhaps, the slightest hint of awe.

But nothing like the awe he felt.

Angelique turned to him and said *Welcome to the Palace of Thought* except she didn't move her lips. The words were clear in Bill's mind but he was nonplussed by this latest revelation, that these beings had no need of speech and suddenly his mind was swamped with exclamations of welcome and joy.

It made him feel queasy.

Slowly, the eyes before him took bodily shape, with arms and legs and bodies of different shapes and sizes. Quite normal. Perhaps it was the light that had played tricks, giving each of them a supernatural appearance until his own eyes could adjust, but just as he thought he had returned to familiar ground, a flock of birds swooped into the space between them, all moving in perfect union, uttering a song that added depth and harmony to the chord that was still ringing in his ears.

How very strange, he thought.

Strange? Not strange, came an unspoken reply in his head.

Angelique, who was still watching him, laughed. A sound like a hundred tiny bells.

'This is our, how would you put it, our council? Where we care for the Host and do Her bidding.'

'I see,' Bill lied. It was not what he had expected. 'Which one is the Mother?'

Angelique laughed again.

'The Mother?'

'Yes, you told me I would meet the Mother. Is she here?'

'Of course she is, Bill.'

'Which one?' He looked at the circle of strange beings before him, each bathed in the extraordinary light. Then he returned his gaze to Angelique, giving her the benefit of his juttiest jutting jaw that served as a question mark in its own right.

'You're looking at her,' Angelique replied. 'I am The Mother.'

12

Bill didn't know what to think.

The Mother? An attractive, floaty thing with no *posterior* to talk of? Quite unlike The Chief. And what did she know, what *could* she know? One so young and inexperienced in the day-to-day running of such a complex system.

And yet...

He studied her freckly face with a new understanding. Perhaps she was older than she appeared and had maintained her youthfulness with attitude alone, refusing to bow to the stress of life at the top.

Vitamins ABCDE plus lots of laughing and a little bit of what I really like in life.

Bill heard the words. Again, her lips did not move. He understood.

'So what your Host does affects the way you, er, look?'

Bill, my dear man, I and the Host are One.

This revelation was like a slap in the face. Bill reeled.

'You can't be. You are here to–'

To guide the Host? Yes. To deal with emergencies? Yes, of course. To love the Host? We all do. But above all, To Be One With The Host.

'I don't know what you mean.'

You will. Come. And stop shouting, just think your words. We'll hear you.

Never before had Bill so yearned for his office, with a stray cat that liked digestives and never spoke to him, perhaps a little untidiness and lots of common sense like an evening in The Singing Sphincter with Ahmed. All this colour and light, bright eyes and speech without speaking, was confusing him.

Bollocks to it all, he thought.

What are bollocks? came the reply.

'Sorry,' said Bill, out loud.

It's all right, we know perfectly well what bollocks are. Just teasing.

Bill snorted. He was not enamoured with smart-arse women, but secretly liked their humour in cases such as this. For once, his mind was thinking quickly and mischievously.

'What do you know about bollocks, then?'

Angelique the Mother actually blushed.

'Well,' she said out loud for change, 'you remember when your Host found our Host extremely attractive…?'

It was Bill's turn to blush.

'…How she kept taking her temperature and putting on flimsy night clothes, even stockings and suspenders? How she…'

'That's quite enough!' said Bill, a little more sharply than he intended. He was wrong-footed.

'So you see, we know what they are for. And as for that limp sausage thingy, we all remember when it stood proud and–'

'I said that's ENOUGH!'

Oopsie. A little embarrassed are we? The giggle was thought-sent too.

Bill just wanted to go home. But he remembered that he had been sent on a mission, the Great Explorer out in the Great Beyond, and he told himself he would see it through. With a stiff upper lip.

'Right then,' he said and remembering that he no longer needed to speak out loud, added in his mind: *Right then.*

Right then what?

Right then, I'd better tell you all why I'm here.

There was a collective thought-sigh, as if all of the Council had been waiting for the banter and mischief to stop.

And why are you here?

Why do you think?

Because your Host, Mr Brian, has a problem?

Mr Brian? That sounds so, well, Upstairs Downstairs!

What do you mean?

Oh, nothing. Yes Mr Brian has a problem. We found cancer cells near his liver.

Suddenly, the air was filled with a furious whispering that Bill could not decipher. He knew some of these strange beings were panicking, others remaining calm but discussing the odds of life and death, and one, a rather shrill thought-voice, demanding a second opinion.

It was Angelique The Mother who restored order.

This is nothing unusual. Bill could understand why she was The Mother, such was the commanding tone in her thoughts.

How so? sent Bill, hopefully.

Everyone has cancer cells at some time or other. They can be dealt with. The problem is... Angelique hesitated for a moment. *The problem only occurs when human tests show up cancer cells. We can deal with it, but not when that sharp knife slices into our world or those disgusting chemicals are thrust at us.*

'What...!'

It's what they do. They call it surgery and chemotherapy.

'What's so wrong with that?'

They never give us a chance to show what we can do.

'What would *you* do?'

You mean, what should we tell you to do? You already know the answer.

'Yes, but... but our Host is feeding himself on junk food and...'

Then change his choices for him.

'But we don't know how!'

70

Suddenly there was a flaring light in the periphery of Bill's vision. Someone apart from the Mother had something to say, although Bill had suspected all along that the words he heard in his mind had been coming from everyone present.

I am Persephone, Thought Master of this Host, and I tell you that we are disturbed by what you say. It seems to us that you have no control. Are there intruders where you come from?

Bill thought for a moment, not realising that his thoughts could be heard. *Flukes yes, but we dealt with them, now there are strange folk down at Liver Central, cancer cells nearby. Yes there are intruders but what do we do?*

There is an answer.

These sudden encouraging words came not from Angelique but from Persephone who seemed to have a limited vocabulary.

Make your Host listen to The Mother.

'How?' *Sorry, how?*

Angelique the Mother had the answer. *The Host Brian is a man and therefore he does not listen. He goes to work, he does what he does, and he comes home late when our Host Betty is tired. I know this, because I am tired too come what the humans call "closing time". But we must stop him. Unless we stop him, or more specifically unless you, Bill, stop him, he will die, and if he dies, we – our Host, myself – will be heartbroken and as a result we too are in danger of attacks from without.*

This time she did not giggle and Bill thought she looked much older.

'I understand,' he said, then concentrated on the new method of communication he was learning. *I understand, but what I don't know is how to change all this. I mean, our Host has a demanding job and if he doesn't do it, what happens to your host when the money stops and she can't go to the Women's Institute, can't give money to charity, and can't afford her circle of friends? Tell me, what should we do?*

The reply came after a few minutes of contemplation.

Money isn't everything.

'Oh but it is!' Bill forgot himself and shouted. 'How can your Host live without pearls, weekly visits to the hair-dresser, money in her pocket for her lunches with friends at Sheldrake Manor, those magnificent dresses, presents for the grandchildren. And what about Christmas? Do you know how much that set us back last December? It was outrageous!'

She doesn't even like those things.

'Then why does she do it, week in, week out, year in year out?'

Because it is expected of her.

'Expected? Expected! If my Host dies…'

May we remind you why you are here?

Bill took a deep breath and calmed himself.

I am here because you can help us.

A murmur went around the Mansion, the light visibly increasing.

But what I want to know, what I need to know, is how you can help us?

72

There was a silence that lasted a full minute during which thoughts flashed faster than Bill could catch. He was about to yell at them all, tell them to stop behaving like a bunch of delusional women, when suddenly the air stilled and the thoughts stopped their manic flashing to and fro.

Prepare blueprint download, came Angelique's command.

13

'You're familiar with the ear as a means of exit?'

Bill was offended. But it was, after all, a true enough statement. Though he no longer had his coil of rope. That, hopefully, remained attached to the Host's ear and would still be there when he returned.

He looked at Angelique the Mother and realised he didn't want to go back. Even though it was clearly his duty to do so.

'Yes,' he said. 'Can't you come with me?'

'No.'

'But you could…' Bill realised he was about to speak from his heart, something he rarely did. 'But you could help us.'

Angelique held up the tiny download.

'This,' she said solemnly, 'will guide you. It is the biorhythm program that we use here. Our Host is not immune to the same problems that beset your Host, but she knows deep down how to deal with anything, however frightening. She takes care to ensure that food is her medicine and her medicine is her food, she accepts everything with gratitude and she laughs a lot.'

Bill felt his face darkening. 'You're losing me.'

'How do you think she dealt with the menopause?'

'The what…?'

Angelique gave him her cutest smile. 'Of course, the meno-pause is not something you would be familiar with. Though it would have helped if you *had* understood when our Host went through those panic attacks some years back.'

'Oh yes, those.' Bill remembered the chaos when his Host had yelled at his wife instead of trying to understand.

'And the night sweats?'

'Okay, okay,' said Bill, hoping Angelique wouldn't get on to the subject of libido and vaginal dryness. 'But now that we know what to do about the menopause…'

'It's a bit late now. I think it's called shutting the gate after the horse has bolted. Anyway, it's no longer a problem be-cause Our Lady is serene, a rose in full bloom, surrounded only by sweet fragrances.'

'How very… very *female*,' retorted Bill, instantly regretting it.

Angelique straightened the folds in her silky dress. 'Indeed, very female as you put it, and probably the only hope your stubborn Host has of remaining alive for more than a few years.'

Bill wanted to argue, but he knew she was right. 'So we plug this in to the mainframe, and then what?'

'Quite simple really. Those cancer cells cannot survive if you starve them.'

'You mean our Host has to stop eating?'

'No, silly. He just has to stop eating *crap*.'

76

Bill was shocked.

But before he could ask *what crap?* she went on: 'And eat healthy. And change his lifestyle. And his job.'

'His job? What about the money?'

'We told you, the money isn't important.'

'But the mortgage? The children? The grandchildren? The car, the caravan, the holidays?'

Angelique shook her head as if Bill was being a numbskull. 'Let me tell you something, Bill. When we sensed your coming, I came myself to greet you because at last we thought we had the answer to our prayers. A hero, a great adventurer, leaving his Host to face all the dangers that we know are out there, to come to see us and find answers to a very grave problem.'

He brightened and puffed out his chest.

'But,' she added solemnly, 'you appear to be something of a disappointment.'

His shoulders sagged. She gave him an intense look that, despite her freckles and an endearing little nose, shone with a strength of character that Bill could not help but admire.

Suddenly, the stern look melted and she smiled. 'You need proof, don't you?'

The scientist in Bill nodded.

'Typical man. Come with me.'

Once again she took his hand and coaxed him towards a darker opening that Bill sensed led away from the Mansion of Love, a term that he was frankly tiring of, into a passage-way lit by candles. He half expected to see more furry animals, but was disappointed. Soon, they entered a room that would be better described as a cave than any kind of useful habitation, lit by more flickering candles and, Bill noted with a little disappointment, an absence of ethereal music.

Angelique knelt before a bulbous extrusion that looked like melted candle wax that had dripped down the wall, forming an altar-shaped mass upon which more candles burned to give off a pleasant aroma of spices and herbs.

She didn't let go of his hand so Bill knelt next to her.

'What's this then?' he asked, his voice echoing intrusively.

'Sshhh. Listen to my thoughts.' *Just a short while, because you have to leave before earth's dawn.*

Okay. I'm listening.

Your Host was not the first.

What do you mean?

There was a brain tumour here.

What? Right here? Bill tried to rise as if he should leave the scene of such horror, but Angelique held him firm.

Right here. Look at it, what do you see?

Dead cells. Like there has been some kind of holocaust in here. But somehow you have made it beautiful. A shrine.

Indeed it is a shrine. But there was a time when we feared for our lives. It was horrible, a mass of writhing rogue cells, a nest of terror.

What do you mean?

78

There were strange creatures here. Persephone found them and wanted to stand and fight because she knew they were not natural. She almost died. She is so innocent. But thank the gods she came and found me, because together, the two of us – with the support of everyone else – we fought with everything we could muster.

How awful. It must have been hell.

Yes. A tear ran down Angelique's cheek. *We thought it was the end. We were panicking. One of the brain workers came in and saw what was going on, and ran around screaming for two days. The pain was horrible. The Host was in agony, popping pills every half hour, and we thought we were all going to die.*

Bill's shoulders slumped, feeling the agony. He recalled the time his own host had an ingrown toenail, the first time he had ever had to travel south, and the incredible fight with all those evil puss cells and the heat from such infernal inflammation.

What did you do?

Angelique sobbed. Bill's heart went out to her. He put a tentative arm around her shoulder and had an immediate erection.

We embraced it.

Eh? Bill dropped his arm, confused.

We didn't know what else to do. We surrounded it all with our love and... and prayed... I guess.

Fat lot of good that does. Bill's jaw was jutting again.

Well it worked. Kind of. It was while we were all there, arms round each other hugging this horrid thing when someone asked why the blood in the surrounding veins was so, well, so weak and translucent.

Sounds like you were lacking in white cells.

Yes, but we didn't know it then.

What did you do?

Exactly what you are going to do when you get back to–

'To my own host?' Bill suggested out loud.

'Yes,' confirmed Angelique. 'Go now. Trust the download.'

Bill hesitated, then bent and kissed her gently on the lips.

I'll be back, he thought, but he wasn't sure she heard him.

14

Bill had no idea how to climb up a rope. Descending had been hard enough.

The Host, who was sleeping peacefully if noisily, had turned over again and by some miracle his rope was still attached to the same ear through which he had climbed.

He stared at the damn thing for an age through his light enhancing goggles, then tried to wrap his arms and legs around it, cursing as he slid uncomfortably to land on his posterior.

Eventually he remembered the radio.

'Hullooo. Come in. Anyone there? This is Bill. I'm back. Over.'

Nothing. Just a hiss.

He repeated his call several times, adding S.O.S. for good measure.

'… ill … sat … ooo?'

The fragments sounded vaguely like Ahmed.

'Repeat please. Ahmed is that you? Repeat dammit. Over'

'… ook up … all in … ere … tingfor … ooo … ver.'

Hook up? Bill thought? Or look up? He looked up. In the gloom he thought he could make out a face.

'Ahmed, if that's you up there, throw down a manual on how to climb a rope. Over.'

'… oh knee … eye … taround … ooo.'

'What the…' Bill let go of the switch and thought for a minute, not his strongest suit. The penny dropped. "No need, tie it around you".

Aha.

'You going to pull me up then? All by yourself? Over.'

Instead of a crackly reply he heard a shrill whistle from above. He looked up. This time he thought he could see three faces peering down. One of them appeared to be waving and yelling, "We'll pull you up you dumb jackass" but the voice was so faint it could have been something far more complimentary.

Bill tied the rope under his armpits. He gave a tug, sending a terse 'Ready. Over.'

The pain was excruciating, but he edged up the craggy cliff face inch by inch until he could make out the faces of Ahmed, Digby and Isabella. Digby seemed to be doing more directing than pulling, while Ahmed heaved manfully and Isabella revealed astonishing strength in her shoulders and upper arms.

Eventually he was able to get an arm around a hair that was mere fluff to the Host but a pillar of towering strength to Bill.

'Hello everyone,' Bill beamed, although what the three rescuers saw was more of a deadly grimace thanks to the goggle strap and the tightening of his skin.

'Ugghh, let him go. He's finished,' said Digby, unkindly.

Bill whipped off the goggles, remembering the effect they had on The Mother. This time the smile worked a little.

Isabella took his painful face in her hands and kissed him. 'Our hero. Welcome home,' she breathed.

'Drop him, I say,' said Digby, rolling his eyes.

Ahmed reached out a hand, pulled him over the precipice and embraced him.

'Good to have you back,' he said, then remembered himself and stepped back. 'The Chief's waiting for your report.'

No feet-up-bottle-of-port-and-a-cigar for me then, thought Bill, and sighed with pleasure at being the returning hero.

'Tell us about the nymph,' said Digby. 'No details omitted.'

'Ma'am, I did NOT enter a nymph.' Bill was close to losing his temper.

The Chief gave him a withering look that might have said "I want to believe you" but was closer to "What the devil have you been up to?".

'Your message said something about going into a nymph!'

'What I said was… oh, never mind.'

Bill rummaged in his pockets for the download. It took him a while to locate it among the maps, torch, water bottle, scissors, string, sticking plasters, bits of torn hanky, hip flask and crumbled digestives, but eventually he triumphantly held up the tiny drive.

'What's that?' asked Imelda.

Digby volunteered an answer. 'It's our doom. A virus download. Throw it out now.'

'Might be porn,' said Isabella hopefully, 'after all, he's been messing around with nymphs.'

'OUT,' yelled The Chief, 'all of you, now.'

'But…' began Digby.

'I said OUT!'

All three turned to leave, despondent.

'Not you, Ahmed.'

Digby was indignant and turned to his boss. 'Why should he stay. We all need to know what's going on.'

'Need I remind you that Ahmed's division is the one under threat? Anything Bill here has found out impacts directly on him. Now go, and if I have need of your supposed knowledge of technology, I'll send for you.'

Isabella dragged Digby from The Chief's office.

'Now then,' sighed Imelda, 'what do we do with this… this what-you-call thing?'

'Plug it in somewhere, I guess,' said Bill helpfully.

'Give it to me.' Ahmed stepped forward and took the download. He pulled out a palm-sized device and pushed the flat end of the download into the side. A small screen flickered into life and the three of them peered at it.

'PLEASE WAIT – UPLOADING. ESTIMATED TIME 5 MINS.'

They watched a set of tramlines fill slowly with blue while a twirling disk told them something was about to happen.

Then the screen went blank.

'Uh-oh,' breathed The Chief. 'Perhaps Digby should have stayed.'

'It's OK,' said Ahmed. 'Just wait.'

'Hope it's OK,' said Bill.

A message appeared. 'This file is not from a trusted source,' it said. 'Are you sure you want to proceed?'

Both The Chief and Ahmed looked at Bill suspiciously.

'Well?' they said in unison.

Bill nodded, a lump in his throat. He sure as hell trusted Angelique. He actually thought he was in love with her.

'Do you want me to go back and ask them?' he said sheepishly.

'Bugger that,' said Ahmed and stabbed the "YES" panel.

The tiny screen burst into life. It had a seductive rainbow background and flowers floated across it. With the odd multicoloured butterfly.

And in the middle were the words:

WHEN ALL ELSE FAILS, TRY SOMETHING. CLICK TO CONTINUE.

15

'Try *what*, exactly?'

The Chief's face was not a picture of confidence.

Ahmed scrolled down with a flick of a finger.

On the Nature of Cancerous Tumours and their Treatment, said the screen in Verdana Bold 24 point with a yellow highlight. Then, in smaller italics: *Report by Angelique St John Stephens Arabesque, Mother of The Betty Davis Protectorate, and Persephone Yinyang, Thought Master.*

'My, my,' exclaimed Imelda, 'they do have funny names over there. Very exotic.'

'Perhaps we should use our second names too?' suggested Bill. 'On second thoughts,' added Bill Jones, 'they are a bit boring, so maybe not.'

'Let's move on, shall we?' urged Imelda Stiff and Ahmed bin Laden made a conscious decision to keep quiet. He thumbed to the introduction.

There are two vital aspects to wellbeing and the denial of foreign invaders within The Host (TH), they read silently, Bill and Imelda peering over Ahmed's shoulders, ignoring the faint odour of spices. *One, Positive Biorhythms (PB) must be maintained and even enhanced. Two, because cancer cells (CC) react vigorously to sound waves, all commu-*

nication in their proximity must be conducted by MindSpeak (MS).

'By *what?*' exclaimed Imelda.

'MindSpeak. Talking without moving your lips,' said Bill. 'They do it rather well over there.'

'Do they now,' snorted Imelda, 'all a bit Sci-Fi don't you think?'

Bill didn't answer because he was reading the next paragraph.

Neither PBs nor MS are any use at all without Attitude Shift (AS) as CCs feed on Junk Food (JF). Thus we get $TH + (CC+JF) - (PB+MS) = CD$ where CD represents Certain Death.

'Oh bugger,' said Bill. 'Never was any good at algebra but that looks like bad news.'

Imelda's face came over all blotchy and Ahmed seemed as pale as his dark skin would allow.

'On the other hand,' Bill said, visibly brightening, 'they did manage to conquer a brain tumour between them.'

'Now you tell us,' scolded Imelda. 'Can't we skip all this formula stuff and get to the nitty gritty?'

Ahmed obeyed, scrolling furiously until he found a section headlined CONCLUSION.

Influences come from within the mind of The Host, Ahmed read out loud, *and from external sources, namely television, the wireless, newspapers, books and conversations, and are therefore largely negative in nature and add considerably to the chances of CD.*

'Might as well plan the funeral now,' said Imelda.

Bill turned to her with a look of disbelief. 'Ma'am?' he said mainly for Ahmed's benefit. He restrained himself from playing with a lock of her hair as a token of sympathy. 'Ma'am, that is most unlike you, if I may say so.'

Blushing, Imelda looked into his eyes which she thought seemed older and wiser. 'Is she anything like me?' she asked.

'She…?'

'Betty's Chief. This Mother person.'

'Oh no, she's—' Bill restrained himself. 'Compared with you, Ma'am, she's an airhead.'

Imelda smiled and commanded Ahmed to read on.

So the priority must be no JF under any circumstances on pain of death, maximum PB and MS at all times. AS can only be achieved by the input of the nearest and dearest which was difficult in our case and required the intervention of a friend (see Appendix 8).

'Nearest and dearest,' echoed Imelda. 'How quaint.'

'Yes, quaint indeed,' said Ahmed, 'but obviously our Host didn't serve the purpose on this occasion.'

Bill, one step ahead thanks to his recent adventure, immediately chipped in: 'Scroll down to Appendix 8 and let's see who came to the rescue while our Host was trying to earn a living.'

Ahmed's thumb worked furiously across the screen.

Hyacinth Bradford, b 1984 Nepal, author.

'A hippy,' observed Imelda.

'Hippy or no, she may have saved at least one life so far, maybe two if we read on.' By now Bill was prepared to believe in anything and anyone.

Studied philosophy at Beijing University 2002-5.

'Now we're getting somewhere,' said Imelda, a little caustically.

m. Gregory Soames 64, now Lord Watford.

'Oh... my... God.' Imelda seemed to go blotchy again. 'The dirty old man.'

Bill couldn't help himself. 'What's wrong with that? Who says a man shouldn't have a young wife? Keep him warm on those long winter nights, that kind of thing...'

Imelda gaped at him. 'Bill...?'

'Look at this,' said Ahmed, saving the day. He continued reading.

Admitted Alderhay Hospital June 2007, diagnosed brain tumour, given six months. Wrote "I Will Survive" pub. Sage Books Feb 2008.

'That's about nine months after diagnosis.' Imelda's calculation was spot on. 'What else?'

Dismissed as a delusional fanatic by the medical fraternity, wrote "I'm No Nutcase" pub. Sage Jan 2009.

'Wow!' The exclamation was three-fold.

Attacked by a panel of doctors on "Health Now" (BBC 2, Jan 26 2009). Smiled throughout, attributing successful treatment to PB combined with a diet of beetroot, carrots, spinach and apples plus high dose Vitamin C and a month of winter sunshine in the Caribbean for added Vitamin D. And lots of laughter with best friend Fenella.

'Fat chance of our host doing that,' said Bill. 'Too busy locked away in a darkened room living on a diet of burgers.'

'But if this is true…' began Imelda.

'Better believe it,' interrupted Ahmed. 'There's more…'

Met Our Host at Broad Bean Organics in High Street, Watford when our Mastercard was rejected at checkout. Offered to pay for assorted organic vegetables and a bottle of Biotta carrot juice. Ensuing conversation about headaches and a general feelings of weariness led to the sharing of herbal infusion in the shop's café and the rest, as they say, is history.

'So our Host's wife…' Imelda began.

'Knows there's a solution,' finished Ahmed.

Which leaves one Big Question, thought Bill.

'Pardon?' said Imelda, 'what did you say?'

'I didn't,' said Bill, thinking his next sentence: *How do we get our Host to listen?*

All three were silent for a few moments. Then, within their reflection on the dilemma they faced, both Ahmed and Bill distinctly heard a voice in their minds.

PB plus MS plus AS, Imelda was thinking.

Are we doing MS? They thought in unison.

Sure are, replied Imelda and gave a huge MindSpeak smile.

16

It was a curtailed thought-smile because before the three could congratulate each other on such an astounding breakthrough, the alarms sounded. A dreadful wailing sound accompanied by flashing red lights on the console so long ignored by The Chief and her senior officers.

They looked at each other.

Bill was the first to react, striding to the console on his long, thin legs then jutting his jaw at it while eyeing the mass of winking lights and screen messages.

'It's Liver Central,' he reported and Ahmed was at his side in an instant.

'Some kind of attack?' he asked in worried tones, flicking switches and stabbing buttons.

'Leave that alone,' said Imelda in her most commanding tone. 'It's meant to be For My Eyes Only.'

'Yes, but something terrible must be happening,' said Bill.

'I'd better go,' cut in Ahmed.

'Wait!' Imelda was not The Chief without reason. 'First we find out what the problem is.'

'Can you get a visual?' Ahmed sounded desperate: he had been away too long.

'I think so,' said Imelda, studying the console. 'It's this pretty knob here if memory serves.'

Suddenly the whole room lurched and there was a terrible groaning sound from the depths below their feet. It sounded like a rhino in its death throes.

'Shit,' said Ahmed, clinging to the console's metal rim.

'Precisely,' said Bill sarcastically, clinging to Ahmed.

'The squits more like,' added Imelda and, while furiously working at the controls to get a picture, confirmed her Chiefly insights: 'Just proves that Liver Central is under attack.'

The groaning turned to something more anguished, somewhere between a sperm whale giving birth and a tower block collapsing. All of the windows shattered as the room seemed to twist. Bill didn't even notice Imelda's heavy bosom crush into his chest because he was trying to focus on the image on the console screen.

'What the–'

A monstrous creature was slithering away from a camera that must have been mounted somewhere near Liver Central. It was dark and scaly, with tentacles that seemed to have suction heads and was shredding the tunnel's walls as it went. Then, as the three watched, it turned its toad-like head towards the camera, a silvery tongue licking over thin, scaly lips.

'That,' breathed Ahmed as he turned for the door, 'does not belong in Liver Central.'

'I'm coming with you,' said Bill. 'This is a job for IFOO.'

No one said "Bless You" but Imelda thought-shouted after the two men as they dashed from her office.

I'll stay here and send what reinforcements I can. Good luck...

'We need body armour and weapons,' said Bill breathlessly as he tried to keep up with the much younger Ahmed. 'Didn't like the look of that dragon.'

'Nadia then?'

'Yes,' Bill agreed, 'Nadia.'

When Nadia saw the anguished look of desperation on Ahmed's face and the grim determination on Bill's, she pulled three of the latest hi-tech suits from stores complete with visored helmets and three packs of VITA-C extruders.

'Should we take guns as well?' Her lively eyes sparkled with a sense of adventure.

'We?' asked Bill.

'Yes, *we*. I'm coming with you. Fed up with this place, full of fat people doing nothing. Who are we fighting then?'

Ahmed smiled at her. 'Wish we knew,' he said, 'though I bet it's something to do with those intruders who were down there a few days ago.'

'Foreigners,' said Bill, knowingly.

'The enemy,' corrected Ahmed.

'Terrorists?' asked Nadia.

Bill and Ahmed nodded.

'Then you'll need me.' She pushed the equipment across the counter and skipped around to their side, stripping her jumper as she came. Bill had a brief glimpse of her firm stomach with a jewelled navel as she divested the woollen garment causing her T-shirt to ride up. She seemed fit enough to him, probably an asset if it came to a fight.

'This is no place for girls,' he said sternly but Nadia gave him a withering glare.

'What you been doing then? Sitting in your office filing a report? C'mon, let's get to work.'

There was nothing Bill could do to stop her as she wiggled into her suit and strapped on a severe-looking black breast-plate with a shimmering blue tinge that had been moulded to fit a woman's form. The helmet gave her an Amazonian appearance. He and Ahmed did the same, Ahmed looking for all the world like a dark lord.

Hesitantly, Bill donned his own helm and flicked the comms link.

'Ready Blue One?'

Ahmed was.

'Blue Two?'

'Ready aye ready,' came Nadia's confident reply. 'Right behind you, Blue Leader.'

Can we trust her? Bill sent by MindSpeak as their BioSys Mark II Bullet-Pod shot southwards in oesophagus drive.

Think so. Not bad looking and seems capable enough for a girl, Ahmed sent back.

I can hear you both, you pair of numnuts!

Bill and Ahmed raised their visors and looked at each other in amazement.

I've been wondering when you so-called executives would cotton on to MindSpeak. And yes, you can trust me even though I'm just a girl!

They turned to look at her, seeing only the blue-black glow in her plex visor and the menacing barrel of her Vita-C extruder. It was Bill who broke the tension.

When did you learn...?

I've always been able to do it. Trouble is, I've never found anyone else who could hear me, except the Spirits.

The Spirits? Bill sighed. He had enough on his hands with evil toad-like creatures assaulting Liver Central, didn't need wacky ghouls and ghosts sending messages to innocent girls like Nadia. Even though she did seem to be most capable and damned attractive.

I call them Spirits. Nadia lifted her visor to give Bill the benefit of her piercing brown eyes. *Only because I can't see them.*

What do they say?

Oh, stuff about the difference between men and women. How men never listen.

The Bullet-Pod's external shields automatically covered the screens as it reached its top speed of 240 peeps making movement within the confined capsule difficult. Bill wanted to scratch his nose but couldn't make his arm obey.

Who do you think they are, then? MindSpeak was easier than normal speech in such conditions that tended to make one appear a little drunk.

How would I know? Nadia wondered if she would be treated like a nutcase but on the other hand here were two men who could actually hear her thoughts. She concentrated on not revealing the way she thought of Bill as a handsome if creaky old man.

Creaky?

Damn.

Ahmed burst out laughing. *You should see his legs. Like a spider with six amputations!*

I have, as it happens, Nadia sent with a snort, *couldn't agree more.*

Bill was flustered but not angry. He knew his limitations. *The Spirits? Who?*

Like I said, how would I know? I like the one called Persephone though.

Persephone? Bill's jaw would have dropped if there was room for a jaw to drop inside the latest plex helmet. *I can tell you all about Persephone–*

Bill would have told Nadia all about Persephone, Thought Master of a Different Host, and Angelique The Mother, both capable of MindSpeak to a degree that put everyone inside this Host to shame.

But he didn't get the chance.

Because right then, as the BioSys Mark II Bullet-Pod flashed south at 240 peeps, Brian Davis of The Poplars, Watford, lost control of all the organs in the region of his liver and

vomited violently, projecting a vile concoction of lager, pea-
nuts, chicken tikka massala and bile salts upwards through
his oesophagus.

Without warning, it hit the Bullet-Pod like a tsunami.

17

The ground moved for Imelda. It heaved and buckled. Her office was all but destroyed in the eruption, her comms system annihilated, sparking its last semblance of life in a pile of dusty, twisted cables, lifeless bulbs and a screen that died with a shrinking pinprick of light that could have been saying "Goodnight Chief".

She felt very ill and very alone.

'Oh Shit,' she breathed, and wondered what it must be like for Bill so far below from whence the powerful upchuck had originated.

'Oh, shit shit SHIT!'

I beg your pardon?

Imelda blinked, and shook her head. And listened. Within her mind.

I said, I beg your pardon?

Who… who's this? Imelda was stammer-thinking, something she normally only did on the back of a decent bottle of Chablis.

I am Angelique. Who FarSpeaks?

Imelda's mind-shutters went up faster than a proud housewife reacting to a sudden storm.

Clear off. I'm busy with a crisis, she said more to herself than to whoever was attempting to break into her world at an inopportune moment.

What kind of crisis? The reply had not been blocked by Imelda's defences. *Can I help?*

Imelda, whose world had been rocked beyond the norm since Bill's return, decided on a policy of honesty.

Unless you know anything about toad monsters, the worst squits we've ever seen, an attack on Liver Central and puke like it's World War Ten, then I suggest you leave well alone.

There was a moment's silence, then: *You're Imelda aren't you? The Chief...?*

I am.

I think I can help. I am The Mother.

For a moment Imelda felt incredibly vicious, not identifying the feelings of jealousy, but still wanting to give this bitch a piece of her mind. But she took a deep breath and sent:

Pleased to meet you, so to speak. How can you help?

Angelique's next thoughts sounded uncharacteristically uncertain. *We do not know of these, ah, toad monsters I think you called them. Can you describe them?*

Imelda outlined the ghastly images they had seen on her monitor before losing contact.

So they are not attached in any way to the body? asked Angelique.

No.

Then they are mutant intruders and if they got in to your host's body, they can be expelled.

How?

Who do you have in the area that you can trust?

Bill. You've met him. And Ahmed, my Liver Central foreman. They're on their way now. If they haven't been wiped out by that puke-storm, thought Imelda, forgetting that the Mother could hear her thoughts.

We have to move fast. At last a hint of urgency. *If we don't deal with this quickly, our Host will have your Host in hospital quicker than you can say "ambulance".*

Maybe not a bad idea.

But if we can deal with it first...

Like I said, sent Imelda testily, *how?*

By using your new thought speech to transmit Positive Biorhythms throughout your Host. And by laughing in the face of Death.

Imelda deemed that last remark unworthy of a reply.

The scene in the bathroom of 16 The Poplars, Watford, would not have been uncommon if it was playing out between two 21-year-old newlyweds who had overdone a Saturday night of binge drinking.

But this was a bathroom tiled in avocado in 1970, ripped apart when Betty Davis read an article in *Ideal Home* in 1985, retiled in white with a plain burgundy dado although the bath and toilet remained in original avocado. It would have been enough to make anyone quite ill, but by 2002

103

plain white, standalone, claw-footed baths were all the rage. However the workmen had chipped three tiles and a section of dado so the whole bathroom had been redecorated to include scenes from *Alice in Wonderland* and a dado in avocado which had returned to fashion thanks to an article in The Sunday Times *Style* section by Megan Maranella.

What was unusual, however, was the sight of a sixty-three-year-old man heaving the last remnants of a chicken tikka massala into The Big White Telephone – in this case a stylish low-level Armitage Shanks – while his wife sat on the wickerwork linen basket next to him and laughed.

'Aarrghh,' said Brian Davis, spitting a piece of undigested chicken gristle into the bowl where it nestled within an orangey-brown concoction that stank worse than a dustbin left to fester because the refuse-collectors were on strike again.

'Tee-hee. That'll teach you,' chuckled Betty, who knew there was something seriously wrong with her husband of forty years but for some reason couldn't stop laughing.

'Shaddapp,' protested Brian, and heaved again.

This only made Betty cackle all the more. She couldn't understand why; somewhere in the corner of her mind she recalled she was seriously considering calling an ambulance.

'I'm dying,' coughed Brian. 'Help me.'

'Do you think St Peter will let you in?' Betty almost collapsed in laughter at the thought. 'You, an accountant, and them lot with all their tax dodges in the name of charity? Give me a break!'

She quite surprised herself with that comment and slapped Brian on the back. He coughed up black phlegm.

'Hurry up and die then sweetheart,' she giggled, 'I can pay off the mortgage with the insurance.'

Brian Davis ignored her. A man's mind always concentrates on the job in hand. And he needed to excrete from the other end next.

Phase One succeeding, sent Angelique, *Phase Two on my mark.*

Betty Davis felt compelled to fetch a two-litre bottle of Highland Spring mineral water. She unscrewed the cap and handed it to her husband who had large beads of sweat forming on his forehead. She began to say, 'Just pretend it's gin,' but Brian Davis seemed barely conscious.

Imelda sent: *Come in, Bill, Phase Two is beginning.* There was no reply from Bill and she hoped beyond hope he had exited the oesophagus in time to avoid the torrent that was coming.

Action Flush!

With his wife's help, Brian Davis tipped the bottle to his crusty lips and drank.

Bill oh Dear Bill if you can hear me, the water's coming and if this works it will flush those BASTARDS through the liver into the duodenal canal and that's where you can trap them please be careful take care show them no mercy and come back to me...

She was rudely interrupted by the combined thoughts of Angelique and Persephone in unison: *More Water!*

Imelda pulled herself together. She was The Chief. If anything happened to The Host it would be all her fault. She must be strong.

Just then there was a *Rap Rap Rap* at the office door and Digby burst in, followed by the head of SCABS, Isabella, who was dressed in a tight black miniskirt and pink tankini top.

'What's going on?' demanded Digby, showering dandruff as he shook his silver hair flamboyantly to emphasise the question. He was wearing his ubiquitous blazer with brass buttons.

But Imelda was immersed in her MindSpeak conversation with Angelique and her desperation concerning Bill's plight. She ignored him.

Can you reach Bill? Mother, Persephone, can you reach him?

Yes... think so... MindSpeak and Positive Biorhythm Broadcast on full power. But it's hell down there. Better get reinforcements ready.

Imelda snapped out of her MindSpeak mode.

'Ah Digby, Isabella. You're just in time.'

'What do you mean?' asked a shocked Digby who was struggling to understand the strange atmosphere.

'Yes, what do you mean?' pouted Isabella prettily.

'Come with me,' snapped Imelda. 'There's a war going on down there, and you're needed!'

'Coming where? At least let me change my clothes. Do you know how much this blazer cost...?'

'Sod that and fall in behind me,' commanded Imelda. 'We're going to save The Host.'

The door fell off its hinges before she could reach it, loosened by a long after-shock that sounded like a dozen piglets closing in on their lunch. Imelda hesitated and then, scratching her head in a manner indicating a Now-Where-Did-I-Put-It-Moment, pulled open a cupboard marked First Aid and rummaged among the dusty packets and bottles as Digby and Isabella watched, bemused.

She found what she was looking for at the back, pulled out the small brown bottle and turned triumphantly to Digby. She took hold of his tie, a natty green number patterned with blue-and-gold portcullises, and with it wiped the dust from the bottle.

Digby protested but Imelda ignored him as she read the label:

Postlethwaite's Tincture of Tamarind

Nuclear Strength

Extreme Caution – Use Sparingly

18

Bill, Ahmed and Nadia had been through hell and back. Literally.

First they had been thrust in a direction they assumed was upwards when hit by the full force of the remaining contents of the Host's voiding stomach.

Then they had been washed south by cascading torrents of water carrying rock-sized peanut particles and what appeared to be giant chunks of carrot.

During this disorienting upheaval, their BioSys Mark II Bullet-Pod had remained intact, probably thanks to the automatic screens, but it had not survived being thrust into the lounge bar of *The Singing Sphincter* at a far higher speed than its designers had ever intended.

It wasn't hard to climb out of the cockpit because the Pod had been ripped open to the elements on impact with Lord Ted's pride and joy, The Copper Bar, which not long before had supported pumps for Gut Wrencher, Padre's Pardon, Liver Purger and Fatima's Flush.

Bill wiped himself down. Ahmed removed a piece of paper that had stuck to his nose, absently noting that it was his own bar tab. He screwed it up and disposed of it. Nadia looked around in the sort of dazed air reserved for women who find themselves in an establishment not originally intended for their patronage.

And Lord Ted emerged from beneath a pile of bricks and two-by-fours with the sort of cursing that confirmed to Nadia that she was in the wrong place at the wrong time.

'The usual please, Ted,' said Ahmed.

'Piss off,' replied Lord Ted, pulling a dangerous-looking piece of electricity cable from his beard.

'My God,' gasped Bill, looking around. 'Did we do all this?'

The Singing Sphincter was a shambolic mass of broken beams and twisted metal. There was even worse damage beyond.

'You bet,' said the Landlord, always one to think ahead where insurance claims were concerned. 'Haven't seen damage like this since Liver Central beat Colon United six-nil in the Cup. Do you want to pay now or wait for the court case?'

Ahmed, who had noted enormous pieces of carrot and peanut in the lounge bar, not to mention a torrent of dirty water flooding across the floor, put the fiasco into perspective.

'So you survived The Host's unfortunate date with the toilet? The worst puke storm in living memory? The flushing floods of water? This place must have been built like a brick shithouse, if you'll excuse the reference…'

Lord Ted held up his hands in surrender. 'Okay, okay, we did have a spot of bother like you say, but nothing compared with a bloody spaceship crashing through your front door!'

His outburst was interrupted by Nadia activating her Vita-C extruder with an ominous double click.

'We've got toads, devils and dragons to deal with,' she said, making Bill go quite weak at the knees, 'and I'm not hanging around here making polite backchat.' She turned for the door, or at least the space where there was once a door.

110

Bill felt he owed Lord Ted an explanation. 'Sorry about all this,' he told the red-faced landlord. 'But Nadia is right. There's big trouble afoot, and we've got to go.'

Bill and Ahmed followed Nadia into the darkness beyond.

'Wait,' cried Lord Ted, 'I'm coming too.'

Clambering over the rubble, slipping on puddles of slime, he joined an adventure that no self-respecting landlord should ever consider, even in his darkest hour.

Ahmed was on point as they entered the upper duodenal gate. It was, he had insisted, his territory and if any damn terrorists were going to mess with his section they'd have him to reckon with first.

The message had been clear. *Enemy flushed south, expected to regroup and enter via duodenal lower gate.* How Persephone, The Mother and The Chief had known this was anybody's guess, but these were strange times.

Ahmed gave the "lie low" signal and Bill sent: *In position. Latest Intel?*

There were distant rumblings that could have come from any of the organs around them. Bill hoped that the digestive explosions were over, at least for now.

None, came Persephone's distant thought. *Be ready,* was Imelda's closer and more powerful, if a little pointless command.

Where are you, Chief? At the back of Bill's mind was the thought that it would help to know where their allies were.

No idea. Never been here before.

Just like a woman. Don't give her a map, thought Bill, we'd all be lost.

I heard that!

Bill was about to send an apology when he sensed movement below. Ahmed and Nadia tensed. They would have edged deeper into the duodenal recess where they waited if it hadn't been filled with a black, sticky goo.

All three aimed their Vita-C extruders. Behind them, Lord Ted took a slug from his hip flask.

'Wait till you see the whites of their eyes,' whispered Bill, not bothering with MindSpeak for once.

'Somehow I doubt their eyes are white,' replied Nadia.

'Red eyes I can recognise,' said Lord Ted, 'I don't see many bright white eyes in my line.'

Only Ahmed laughed, but it was distinctly nervous because now they could see shadows shifting towards them.

'Here they come,' said Ahmed. 'Ready?'

In the confined space below the tentacles seemed to twist together as they hauled themselves back towards the liver from whence they had been flushed. Flat scaly heads, blinking eyes that seemed to glow deep red. Impossible to tell how many, but certainly three or four.

Bill wanted to run, but he forced himself to look at those eyes and he realised, with dread certainty, that those were the eyes of the workmen he had seen during his last visit to Liver Central, only now these creatures did not carry shovels and pretend to be doing a simple clearing task. These were devils bent on destruction.

112

And we have to stop them.

He jutted his jaw and fingered the Vita-C extruder's trigger.

You will.

He thought it was The Chief who sent that, but had no time to reflect on her confidence as the creatures spotted the ambush.

They slithered onwards and upwards.

The Battle for Brian was about to begin.

19

Ahmed fired first. Perhaps it was his patriotism for his beloved Liver Central that made him act prematurely.

A jet of pure vitamin C shot from his extruder as he shouted *'Take that you bastards'*, and a split-second later both Bill and Nadia opened up. Lord Ted cowered behind them, covering his eyes.

The monsters were halted in their advance by that first onslaught. The pure nutrient stung their eyes and forced them to retract destructive tentacles. But after that first unexpected shock their twisted brains told them they were not dead and on they came with deadly intent.

Neither Bill nor Ahmed, nor Nadia, had considered how much ammunition a Vita-C extruder contained. They held finger to trigger as the monsters writhed but advanced.

'Need a sodding gun,' yelled Nadia as she stood and sent a stream of the potent liquid into the eye of an advancing devil. It fell back, but its colleague took the opportunity to extend a tendril that wound around Nadia's midriff. She barely noticed, so intent was she on destroying the enemy in her sights. She was lifted high, still firing.

Bill was angry. He leapt and threw impotent arms around the writhing tendril, feeling its slimy scales, slipping then gaining a better purchase by wrapping his legs around it. He locked ankles and squeezed with all his might. Still the monster held Nadia aloft.

So he bit it.

His mouth was filled with ooze that tasted like rancid butter. Retching, he bit harder. The devil released Nadia with a piercing scream and fixed Bill with the one eye that had not been blinded by the streams of Vita-C. Bill knew he was going to die but he didn't care. He saw the gaping maw advance, ringed with needles of teeth that would mince him like burger meat, and he didn't give a jot.

He sensed the streams of Vita-C dwindle. He yelled obscenities that he wouldn't admit to knowing. He spat at it. And still it advanced.

A small object flew past him and straight into the yawning cavern. It broke at least three needle teeth then spun into the hellish blackness, spewing a golden liquid as it spiralled from view.

The monster screamed, its one eye blinking, and backed away. Three other monsters halted their advance, puzzled.

Dimly in the distance, as Bill dropped from the dripping tendril, he heard Lord Ted's best "Last Orders" voice thunder:

'TAKE THAT YOU BASTARDS!'

They heaved themselves over the threshold and lay panting.

'Did we win?' asked Nadia when she had recovered enough to find breath.

'Did we bollocks,' said Ahmed through gritted teeth. 'They'll come again.'

'Then we fight here,' said Nadia.

Bill summoned the effort to contradict her. 'Who's in charge here?'

'Yeah,' said Lord Ted, 'and who won that round then?'

'Well, we owe you our lives, I admit,' confessed Bill, looking at the rotund landlord with fresh admiration. 'Just what did you throw at it? I thought I was a goner.'

'An antique hipflask fashioned in silver engraved by elven lords from Middle Earth,' said Lord Ted, triumphantly.

'I doubt somehow,' said Ahmed slowly, 'that an elvish hipflask would kill or even slightly injure a monster from hell.'

'Then you haven't read your Tolkein,' replied Ted, who was looking distinctly unlordly.

'So what was in it then?' asked Nadia. 'That might have done the trick.'

'Napoleonic brandy,' said Lord Ted with a self-satisfied smile.

'Aha,' said Bill knowingly, 'heavenly nectar. How come?'

'I've been keeping it for an emergency. Didn't think it would go like this though!'

'Indeed not. But I'm afraid your Napoleonic brandy has met its Waterloo. Look…'

A tentacle was forcing its way through the small entrance that a few moments ago had been wide enough for Bill, Ahmed, Nadia and Ted to squeeze through. But now another tendril joined it, then another. The aperture was forced ever wider.

And these tentacles looked distinctly angry.

'Back,' yelled Bill.

'I'm going to fight them. You can run,' screamed Nadia.

'What will you fight them with?' Bill shouted at her. 'No Vita-C left, no Napoleonic brandy, not even a glass of Niersteiner!'

He grabbed her around the waist and pulled her away from the advancing tendrils just as one was about to capture her again.

Lord Ted was already retreating.

Ahmed spat, and looked at Bill who was holding the struggling Nadia.

'You're right old friend,' he said solemnly. 'This is it.'

'Rearguard action,' said Bill with a stiff upper lip and a look in his eye that said *we've done our best.*

More tentacles came through the aperture, forcing it ever wider, until they could see two or three pairs of red-glowing eyes watching them with evil intent.

Bill held Nadia under one arm while Ahmed ushered Lord Ted down the tunnel away from the danger. He watched over his shoulder as he too retreated. He mulled over the word "retreat" as he went. *Dammit,* he thought, *I'm not the type to retreat...*

Neither am I, thought-screamed Nadia as she continued to kick and struggle, biting Bill's arm.

Bill dropped her.

'Right, you lily-livered old man, we fight right here,' said Nadia defiantly, raising her visor.

'What with?' asked Bill weakly, raising his too.

'Let's try laughing at them. See you on the other side.'

Bill smiled and leaned to kiss her.

Their plex helmets clashed and the kiss did not follow as eight tendrils lashed out towards them.

20

Bill was more tired than he had ever felt. He just wanted to collapse and sleep. He would even tolerate the cat of no fixed abode curling on his lap, maybe nibbling at a digestive.

He forced his puny legs to take him backwards, away from these hellish monsters. They came on, eating up more ground, destroying precious cell walls as they came.

They tried rushing the devils. Bill even succeeding in punching one in the eye but it did no good. The monstrous thing just shimmered and blinked, and continued its relentless advance.

Nadia was screaming, Ahmed cursing, Lord Ted weeping. They fought bravely. Right up until their backs were against the crumbled ruin that was once *The Singing Sphincter*.

It was there they chose the place for their last stand. We'll stand here, thought Bill vaguely, all energy drained, not even enough for MindSpeak. Stand here, stand around, stand our ground. He laughed. Out loud.

Nadia, a gleam in her eye, and Ahmed, wearier than he had ever been, laughed with him.

That's right, laugh.

They all heard it and stopped laughing.

I said laugh. I'm coming. And when I come I want to hear you laughing like drains.

Bill wanted to ask the familiar thought-voice how a drain laughed. But he couldn't muster the energy. So with every last fibre, he laughed. *At least I'll die laughing*, he thought.

You're not going to die. I said I'm coming.

'Let's just laugh then,' he said to Nadia, who laughed back at him, a wild, cackling, devil-may-care kind of laugh.

Ahmed joined in. 'Pour me a pint of Padre's Pardon, Ted!' he laughed and Lord Ted chortled.

'Wouldn't you prefer a wee dram of Napoleonic?'

Ahmed laughed all the louder.

The tendrils crept in to the ruin that was *The Singing Sphincter* and sought out Nadia's lovely midriff, Ted's chubby arms, Bill's thin legs and Ahmed's armoured shoulders. They squeezed. The four of them laughed.

Like drains.

And so did Imelda.

The Chief burst through the door that wasn't, scrambled to the top of a pile of rubble as tentacles attempted to wrestle her to the ground, and emitted glorious rays of Positive Biorhythms that forced the enemy to edge backwards.

Then she held aloft her bottle of Tamarind Tincture: Nuclear Strength.

'DIE YOU BASTARDS' she screamed as she poured the contents onto the wreckage at her feet.

* * *

Brian Davis of The Poplars, Watford, rushed back to the familiar Armitage Shanks receptacle. He was not behaving with anything like the class expected of a senior partner at Grimson, Ramsbotham and Davis, chartered accountants. Senior partners never had the squits, certainly not like this.

There was something far more worrying about this latest turn than anything that had happened in the last hour or so. He had felt as though a monstrous hand had reached into his gut, grasped it with an iron grip, and twisted maliciously. When he screamed involuntarily, Betty had dashed for the telephone. He wanted to tell her not to bother with medical assistance but quite frankly he would rather grapple with Giant Haystacks or The Undertaker than face more of this anguish.

He found it vaguely strange that she was laughing like a mad witch as she spoke to the operator.

The explosion that now ripped through his intestines was too much to bear. His head collapsed over the toilet and he wept. Rivers of molten lava shot through his innermost being. He did not have the strength to lift himself the few inches required for the correct procedure.

'Oh God,' was all he could manage although it sounded more like "Oh Gargghhh".

'Oh yes, he's dying all right,' he heard Betty cackle into the telephone.

He couldn't agree more and wished The Big Event would hasten.

With enormous effort he lifted himself and undid his trousers for the fourth time. He swore it wouldn't be necessary to ever hoist them again afterwards, never fiddle-faddle with those damn flies, never have to tighten that belt to the notch that had sufficed for twenty years yet latterly had refused to agree with him, never ever be faced again with the decision to full-flush or half-flush.

He flopped onto the porcelain, his bottom more-or-less targeted, and his head collapsed between his knees.

The grip on his intestines intensified. His stomach seemed to expand beyond the realms of possibility, then just as suddenly contract again. He thought he heard – no he definitely *did* hear – an explosion. The sound reminded him of the thunderstorm last summer that had taken out Watford Football Club, the telephone exchange and Sainsbury's in a single apocalyptic Act of God.

As he passed out, he thought he heard an angel speak.

He would never admit to it, but on reflection many days later, he would swear to himself that a small voice with the volume of a bellowing bull had yelled:

DIE YOU BASTARDS.

21

'Does my bum look big in this?'

Bill wasn't ready for that. Imelda twirled in a hippyish number that hung low over wide hips and sported dazzling purples and pale yellows. It was magnificent.

'Uh? Oh yes, absolutely fabulous!' exclaimed Bill who hadn't been quite himself since the Battle of Liver Central.

'What! So it does look big?' Imelda stopped twirling and fixed him with her most outraged glare.

'What looks big?'

'My bottom...?'

'Oh, your bottom.' Bill struggled. He wasn't very good at this kind of thing. 'It looks just fine and dandy and, if I may say so, so does your dress.'

Imelda smiled and planted a kiss on his cheek just above the untidy beard that had taken over even more of his face in the weeks since The Host's troubles had begun.

'You are a dear,' she said, picking an errant hair from the shoulder of his jacket. 'Might have to smarten you up though, make you look the part for your new job.'

'New job?' He took a step back and eyed The Chief suspiciously. 'But I like being Head of IFOO. I don't know anything else!'

Imelda laughed.

'We'll see. I have just the thing in mind for you. Now that our Host has bucked his ideas up, we're going to take the opportunity to make a few changes for the better.'

Bill frowned. 'But–'

'No "buts" Bill, this is going to be a much happier place now that Mrs Host has got everything under control…'

'You mean that diet of salads and fruit and vegetable juice? Should make life much easier for Ahmed and his LADS. We've still got to be on the lookout for trouble though.'

He hoped he would never again encounter anything quite as terrifying as those monsters and their Last Stand at *The Singing Sphincter*. The feeling of hopelessness as the devils advanced, the impotence of fighting with hands, feet and teeth, the stupidity of laughing in the face of Death. The certainty of annihilation, the fury of their scratching and biting and… and the sheer joy of The Chief's Ultimate Weapon.

Now *that* was something to laugh about.

The raw power had sent them all flying and *The Singing Sphincter* was no more. Bill had landed in a crumpled heap on top of the pub's splintered sign with a dreadful ringing in his ears. He was covered from head to foot in sticky slime which he hoped was all that remained of the intruders.

Looking up he had seen a figure picking its way across the rubble, through a thick mist of nuked digestive juices, only recognisable as The Chief by her enormous bosom and powerful thighs.

She had appeared to be laughing but Bill couldn't hear anything above the ringing sound.

He had shaken his head to clear it, pinched himself to check that he was still alive, and as the ringing dwindled he had called to her.

'The enemy?' he had croaked.

'Down the pan.'

At least that's what he thought she had said, and he had thrown his head back and laughed too.

Nadia, Ahmed and Lord Ted had survived, and together they had advanced through the duodenum into the digestive tract looking for signs of a retreating enemy. There was none.

Down the pan, indeed.

Bill now looked at The Chief with new reverence and admired her new dress again. Truth to tell, her bum did look big but he thought he could love every yard of it. She had proved herself worthy of her lofty role. He would be happy to accept any backwater job she offered him, especially if it *was* a backwater job.

'And now?' he asked her, thinking that he would like to spend more time with her, perhaps go on holiday together…

'And now I'll show you the new Boardroom,' she replied, matching Bill's own inability to spot an opportunity. 'Although I don't think we should call it a Boardroom. More of a Haven of Inspiration.'

His heart sank. Another time, he thought.

Another time? You don't want to see our lovely Boardroom?

'Oops, sorry,' he said out loud. 'I was thinking of something else.'

He took her hand and smiled: 'To the Haven, then.'

The new boardroom did not exactly have a door. By some new method of thought-control part of the wall just faded away to reveal a pleasing array of soft pastel shades and a single chord drifted in the perfumed air, a chord that defied the realms of musical possibility.

There was no large mahogany table. No chairs. Cushions arrayed on a soft carpet, all in matching colours. It seemed a far larger room than the old Boardroom; but then, it wasn't a room, it was a *haven*.

What a presenter on *Escape to the Country* would call "a lovely space".

'You don't want me to be your new interior designer, then,' said Bill sarcastically as he tried to quell the emotions that even a cynical old man feels when confronted with something so undeniably moving.

'Do you like it?' asked Imelda, fishing for complements. 'I had some help, you know.'

'From whom?'

'That download you brought over from next door,' she said happily. 'It wasn't just about how to beat cancer cells, there was a lot of stuff on there about creating a wholesome environment.'

'Oh no,' muttered Bill. 'Talking rats and cats. Give me a break!'

'Perhaps in time, dear. Perhaps in time. For now we've got these.' She pointed to a large flatscreen mounted on what might have been a wall except that it seemed vaguely transparent. She clicked her fingers at it.

When all else fails, try something.

The words floated across the screen.

'Seen it. Done it. Got the T-shirt.' Bill thought he was being cool. But there was more.

We're not generals, we're street fighters.

'Sure are,' he chuckled. 'That was one hell of a street fight. Imelda squeezed his hand.

Laughter is the best medicine. Juicing ain't bad either.

Nature has it covered.

'Ha. Now we get to the nitty gritty. This is new territory for me,' said Bill.

'And for me,' agreed Imelda. 'For all of us. But we can make it happen.'

Beautiful Biorhythms are, well, Beautiful.

Hot dogs are flatliners. So is Chicken Tikka Massala.

'Amen to that,' said Bill and turned to face her. Her soft skin reflected back the pastel colours. She looked quite beautiful to him. He thought he should kiss her now.

But the kiss was not imparted.

'Well, well, well, what have we here?' intruded Digby's gruff voice.

'Que guapa!' squealed Isabella. 'It's lovely!' She was wearing her finest Flamenco.

Not a patch on my Imelda's dress, thought Bill.

Why thank you!

Bill blushed.

Digby bowled into the "space".

'Where do we sit?' he asked.

Imelda waved a regal hand at the cushions. 'Take your pick.'

Ahmed arrived, followed by Nadia whose sheepish look revealed that she felt out of her depth, more accustomed to fighting devilish monsters than entering what to her was a far cry from her Ticket Office and Travel Store.

All of them sat. Digby pushed out the single tail of his magnificent blazer and frowned as he lowered himself. Isabella managed a dignified and stylish curling of the legs and dropped lightly onto a cushion that matched the crimson hues of her dress. Nadia hung back timidly until Bill ushered her towards a chocolate-coloured cushion that matched her eyes.

As Bill and Imelda found their places, Digby was watching the slideshow. **Everybody Needs Somebody** it read as the Biorhythm music changed key. His eyes moistened. 'Sure do,' he mumbled, reaching for Isabella's hand. They let their fingers entwine.

'Now,' said Imelda, fanning her magnificent dress around her, 'first things first. Ahmed?'

Ahmed was the only one still standing. He leaned against what might have been a wall or could have been a force

130

field, arms folded, and let his eyes rest on each of them in turn.

'One thing's for sure,' he said at last. 'Whatever was in that bottle that The Chief brought to the party should be patented. The enemy is defeated, gone, flushed away like the turds they are, hopefully for good.'

There was a ripple of applause and a few murmurs of "Hear Hear".

'But we must be on our guard,' he went on, unfolding his arms and taking a pace forward into the beautiful space. 'There are no more cancer cells in Liver Central. I think they have been flushed away too. All I can say is this. Whatever it was that gave us the victory,' his voice climbed an octave and Bill realised his friend would one day make a great orator, 'we did it together and if there is *ever* a next time, we'll do it together again!'

This time there was cheering and loud applause in the board-space.

'But,' continued Ahmed, his voice now almost a whisper. 'We need a new pub. And we need to pin a medal on the lapel of its good landlord, Lord Ted!'

More applause. Digby, looking thirsty, licked his lips.

Isabella coughed daintily. 'Can this pub stock some nice *Rueda Verdejo?* I do like that with ice and soda.'

'Of course,' said Imelda who seemed to have mastered the ability to combine a mother figure with her all-powerful role within The Protectorate. 'But that aside, I have some important announcements to make.'

Bill sensed this might have something to do with Imelda's revelation that she was about to give him a new job. He

131

wondered whether this might be an opportune moment to stand down and announce his retirement, but he held his tongue and inwardly quailed at what might be coming.

'First,' said Imelda solemnly, 'credit where it's due.'

Digby's chest expanded a couple of inches and he sucked breath to hold in his flabby tummy. Ahmed and Bill did not move, but both realised independently and silently that Nadia had said nothing and sat still as a mouse – a creature to which she bore absolutely no resemblance – not seeking any recognition whatsoever.

But recognition was exactly what she got.

Persephone? Can you hear me? The MindSpeak was all Imelda's.

Sure can. Loud and clear, came Persephone's reply, which they all heard.

At the height of the battle, whose thought messages could you track most easily?

Why, that's easy. Persephone, Thought Master of Mrs Host, seemed to adopt an almost singsong thought pattern. Quite unlike the fast and furious chatter when the tendrils were flying, the Vita-C drying up, and *The Singing Sphincter* collapsing.

Go on.

My dears, there's no one quite so powerful in the MindSpeak department than your warrior-chick, Nadia.

Bill grunted his approval and Ahmed thrust a fist into the air. Digby and Isabella looked at each other as if they were not sure what was going on.

'Nadia dear,' began The Chief with a solemn look, 'would you kindly agree to be our new Thought Master?'

'No way,' she protested. 'I've already got a job and I'm doing it damn well!'

'Too right,' said Bill and Ahmed together.

'But,' continued Imelda, 'there's something more you can do for me. For us. For The Host. We've got so much to learn and so little time to learn it. I'm asking you to channel good thoughts to us and therefore to The Host. We need you to help us fight all the nonsense out there that says a hamburger is nutritional, that genetically modified food is safe, and that if curry has some microwaved spinach in it, it must be good for The Host. I'm asking you to be The Host's conscience around here. What do you say?'

Nadia blinked back tears and shook her head. She looked up at Bill and Ahmed who were willing her to accept.

Eventually, she said softly: 'Okay. If it means that much. But…'

'A but?' interrupted Imelda. 'You're allowed one. Go on.'

'But if this ever happens again I want to fight on the front line…' she looked The Chief in the eye, '… with you.'

The moment that passed between them was laden with mutual admiration.

'You got it,' said Imelda proudly. 'But you do all the yelling and shooting.'

Nadia smiled warmly at her Chief.

'Which brings me to a special announcement,' The Chief continued. 'A very important appointment.'

Bill's toes involuntarily curled. Ahmed dug him in the ribs.

'There is a man,' she began, with an emphasis on the word *man*, 'without whom none of us would have a future. He risked life and limb to find out what we should do, and he was at the *forefront*,' her gaze fell on Digby as she said that word, 'the *forefront* of the defence of Liver Central.' She looked back to Bill. 'This man risked everything to fight the very demons of hell, and when I arrived at the scene I saw a Great Warrior giving his all.'

'Come now,' Bill cut in. 'Ahmed was–'

'Ahmed will be rewarded with a promotion. But I am talking about you, Bill.'

He tried to hide behind his beard and wished he wasn't sitting on a pink cushion.

'So, Bill, I want you to be my new Minister Without Portfolio.'

Bill looked up sharply. 'What the hell does that mean?' He sounded angry, and in a way, he was.

'I mean Bill,' went on The Chief softly while everyone else studied fingernails, toes, brushed away imagined dust particles, 'I mean I want you to help me do my job. When we needed a hero, you were there. It might happen again, and next time I want you at my side. Someone wise. Someone courageous. I need you, Bill.'

Her eyes were moist. So were Bill's.

'Okay,' he said softly.

Everyone cheered. Including Digby, who couldn't help himself in the moment's emotion.

'Good,' said Imelda. 'That's settled then.'

134

But Bill hadn't finished. 'I'll be your Minister Without Portfolio,' he said, rising to his feet because he felt more comfortable standing. 'But who's going to do my job?'

'Can't he do both?' asked Ahmed.

'No way,' said Imelda firmly. 'Recent events have shown us that we need a strong Head of Immigration and Foreign Object Office, which we lovingly call IFOO.'

'Bless you,' said Digby.

Imelda glared at him.

'And,' she added, still looking at him, 'I think we need a new head of New and Interesting Technology.'

'A new NIT,' giggled Isabella. It was Digby's turn to look thunderous.

'That will be Ahmed,' announced The Chief, 'and if he wants to change the name, so be it.'

Ahmed was stunned. But everyone knew he was the right man for the job.

Digby studied the flatscreen across which the words **Never Give Up** floated. He wanted to give up.

'...which leaves us with a vacancy at IFOO,' Imelda was saying. 'Digby, can you do the job?'

Digby looked up so suddenly that dandruff erupted around him.

'Of course,' he said.

'Then you are the new Head of IFOO.'

'Ma'am,' he said respectfully, 'I am your obedient servant.'

'Yes, yes, of course,' said The Chief and winked at Bill.

'But,' said the new Head of IFOO carefully, 'may I change the name? After all, everyone laughs and says "Bless You" when IFOO is mentioned.'

A lot of things suddenly became clear to Bill but he maintained a dignified silence.

'Sure, Digby, have you a suggestion?'

'Yes,' said Digby. 'I've always wondered why don't we simplify it. To Foreign Agency, for example?'

'FA?' asked Ahmed.

'Sweet,' said Nadia.

THE END. FOR NOW.

ABOUT THE AUTHOR

Adam Fox is a pen name. In his other life, Alistair Forrest is an author of Historical Fiction. See www.alistairforrest.com

He also writes a website, www.best-health-juicing.com, with the help of his wife Lynda and several friends in the natural health industry.

He is also a health magazine editor and has been a journalist for many years. He is planning further books in the *Cell Wars* series.

If you enjoyed *Cell Wars*, please tell your friends about it, write an online review and/or send the author a message of encouragement via one of the above websites.

Unfortunately, MindSpeak is not possible at this time.

See over for other books by the same author.

BOOKS BY THE SAME AUTHOR

Libertas (2009) ISBN 978-1906836078 (Paperback and large print) 978-1452321516 (E-Book)

Historical Fiction: Julius Caesar force-marches eight crack legions into Southern Spain where he will fight his last ever battle. Arrayed against him are 13 legions under the Sons of Pompey the Great. Among these is a smart youth who is about to find out what it's like to be on the losing side.

'A fast-moving tale of fortitude, survival and eventual retribution told against the background of Rome's bloody civil war.' – Douglas Jackson, author of *Caligula, Claudius* and *Defender of Rome.*

Goliath (2010) ISBN 978-1452327495 (E-Book)

Historical Fiction: His mother is reviled as a whore, his half-brothers detest him and his employer wants to mess with him. It's his last night as a shepherd in the hill country near Beth Lechem, but he doesn't know it. He's about to be recruited as a spy and his mother will be stoned by an angry mob.

Thus begins the story of David and Goliath as it probably was before the religious scribes got their hands on it. A tale of betrayal, love and impossible odds, not least when young David is pitched into an arena to fight a terrifying bull-headed colossus. An experience that will stand him in good stead when the Philistine army marches into Judah to threaten a disorganised Hebrew rabble.

NOTES

Use these blank pages to write some notes about the health issues raised in this novel. For example:

How often do you eat "fast food" or supermarket ready meals?

Do you think processed and refined foods are good for you?

Why do you think cancer has become so prevalent in the last 50 years?

NB. Some answers, but by no means all, can be found at www.best-health-juicing.com

Lightning Source UK Ltd.
Milton Keynes UK
UKOW051259021111

181357UK00001B/31/P